QUARANTINE

ALONE Series by James Phelan

Chasers
Survivor
Quarantine

QUARANTINE

ALONE

JAMES PHELAN

KENSINGTON PUBLISHING CORP.
www.kensingtonbooks.com

This book is dedicated to the memory of
Sgt. Brett Wood,
a magnificent soldier and a true friend.

From childhood's hour I have not been
As others were; I have not seen
As others saw; I could not bring
My passions from a common spring.
From the same source I have not taken
My sorrow; I could not awaken
My heart to joy at the same tone;
And all I loved, I loved alone.

—from "Alone" by Edgar Allan Poe

1

We buried the snow leopard in the morning. The three of us stood in the mist that came with the winter's dawn, the empty streets of Manhattan as quiet as they'd ever been since the attack. The lonely gray light sucked the color from everything but it was all we had to work by as we dug into the earth. A dark stain of frozen soil covered the animal's mate, who we'd buried just the day before, two lifeless forms in stark contrast to a blanket of fresh white snow.

It was Felicity who insisted on the funeral, not Rachel, the animal's caretaker. Maybe it was Felicity's way to keep me here a bit longer, in the hope I'd change my mind about going; or in the hope that while I stalled here a miracle would come—rescue by whoever was left. Not that we knew who was left, not for certain. That's why I needed to leave the safety of these fortified zoo grounds, yet again. Exploring the unknown was our best chance for survival.

In the snow-leopard enclosure of Central Park Zoo we held a little ceremony of sorts, silent and stoic.

Felicity didn't cry but Rachel did—just falling tears, no sound of sobbing. My two fellow survivors, standing next to me, remembering these beautiful animals that had never done anybody any harm, killed by violent figures in the night, those with an unquenchable bloodlust.

There was a bang-crash of a building coming down, probably nearby on Fifth Avenue.

"That was close," Felicity said, spooked.

I nodded, words obliterated, for the sound had roused all the animals left in the zoo, waking them from their mournful chorus into a symphony of alarm, as if they knew that their tickets out of this life were loosely hanging chads.

"I hate it when they do that," I said, close to Felicity's ear, the cries of the birds and the sea lions assaulting my own. It was like trying to hide from Chasers near a car and setting off the alarm—it drew unwanted attention. In a silent city, we were now clearly in focus. "On such a clear morning, this sound'll carry all through the park . . ."

So far this morning the Chasers had stayed away, as if out of respect for the properly dead. I was kidding myself by thinking that—they didn't need emotions, just as they didn't need normal food or shelter or warmth. At least, that was true of the predatory Chasers, the infected who would hunt you down, the ones who'd survive. Ironically, those whose contagion was wearing off—who were technically getting better, their faculties returning—were worse off. By the time they improved enough to find food and shelter, it would be too late; if the aggressive Chasers didn't pick them off, one by one, the harsh winter would.

If my friend Caleb was one of the weaker kind, I could search him out, look after him. But he was a bloodthirsty Chaser, and there was no reasoning with them, as I knew from experience. The only resolution to a conflict with them was death. Was there *any* hope for Caleb? Probably not. Could I give up on him? No.

My packed bag was on the ground. I'd been ready to bug out of the zoo when the leopard died, but now I had doubts. I felt guilty about wanting to leave. I'd tried my best to calm and soothe Rachel. She'd said harsh words, what I felt might be final words . . . and then all our conviction, on both sides of the debate, came undone with the sudden ceasing of a heartbeat.

How callous that sounds, but that's what it had come to: the death of an animal and what came with that had kept me here.

At the thought of leaving, my body felt weak with exhaustion. This time, I told myself, it would be different. It had to be. All I had been doing these past two weeks since the attack was moving from one false touchstone to the other—from 30 Rock, to Central Park Zoo, to Caleb's bookstore, looking for a safety that was no longer possible, if it ever had been. I told myself I was helping, I was doing good, getting one step closer to escaping, to getting home . . . when all I'd really been doing was retracing my steps. Now I needed to make progress, real progress, before—

Before *what,* exactly? Maybe the uncertainty was the worst part. About twenty percent of New York's cityscape had been destroyed in the initial attack. But every day since then there had been new fires and explosions, buildings falling one by one, here and there, as if to remind us that there was more to come. There was another act—maybe several more—to be played out. They weren't finished with us yet—whoever *they* were.

"You should sleep," Rachel said, jolting me out of my thoughts.

Neither of us had slept in the night and we both had full days ahead. "So should you," I replied.

"I'm not the one going out there," she said.

"I'll be fine."

"Well, at least rest for an hour, then go."

"I can't," I said. "There's no way I can sleep right now."

She wiped the back of her sleeve down her face, her breath fogging in the cold. We watched Felicity trudging towards the main building, heading off to rest. Or maybe she was giving me and Rachel time alone. I got the feeling that Rachel had something she wanted to say to me.

"Rach?"

She looked at me, her eyes wet.

"What's up?"

"Jesse . . . you know it wasn't your fault, right?"

"What wasn't?"

"What happened to Caleb."

"Yeah?" I said, crossing my arms around my chest. "Well, I brought us all together, didn't I?"

"Jesse—"

"I coaxed him into finding out what had happened to his friend, his parents, so I have a right to feel just a little bit responsible."

"Everything—everything you've been doing these past few days has been for us, for our survival."

I'd tried to do the right thing. I'd spent so long denying the reality of events myself I could recognize the same behavior in Caleb. You need to feel it, I told him, remembering that I'd forced him to visit his parents' place. He hadn't been able to express the horrors of what he'd found but it was pretty clear he'd seen more than he needed to. It had reminded him just how much he'd lost—he lost everything; he'd lost it all.

Then I remembered.

"He—he ran to help that fallen soldier last night," I said. "He ran into harm's way, to help a stranger. I— I might have run away from the danger."

"What are you getting at?"

"*He* ran to help. *I* didn't. I didn't know what to do. All I did was run. So when Caleb needed me—when he really needed me—I *failed* him."

"But there's nothing you could have done to prevent it."

Her words hung in the air for a moment and my breath steamed in front of my face as I studied the newly disturbed dark earth and deep snow in front of us.

"You weren't there, Rach."

"It was beyond your control," she said.

"You didn't see that blank look in his eyes. You didn't see him feeding on that dead soldier—*drinking* him, like some kind of wild animal."

"But I know how you feel." She looked at me hard. "Just like what happened to my leopards here; *taken* from me. Could I have stopped it if I were out here that night? No. They would have killed me too."

"Caleb was protecting me, Rach. Don't you see?" I walked around the enclosure. "It could have been me—it *should* have been me, if any of us. *I'm* the one who's been itching to trek out of this damned city. I'm the one always pushing—"

"Jesse—"

"I can't let it go. I can't just forget him, lose hope for him—it's as important to me as . . ."

"As?"

I leaned on a fallen tree that was scarred by big scratch marks from the leopards, and breathed through rising nausea. Rachel put an arm around my shoulder and said softly, "We're going to get through all this. All of us—Caleb too."

I nodded; I wanted to believe.

"He did what you'd do and what we'd do in the situation."

I fought back tears. "You don't know that."

"Of course I do."

She stood close to me, her body warm against mine.

"Thanks," I said. I was glad that she saw it that way. I stood and she hugged me and we walked out towards the central pool.

I paused by the gates to the zoo, and adjusted the straps of my backpack. The weight of the loaded pistol in my coat pocket no longer gave me peace of mind or felt like a burden; it was just there, another appendage in this new world.

"Look, Jesse . . ." She looked sadder in that moment than at any time I'd known her. "I've known for eighteen days that I'd have to walk away from here at some point, leaving them to fend for themselves."

"So that means—"

She looked from the caged animals to me.

"It means, yes, I'm ready."

I smiled.

"Go find that group of survivors down at Chelsea Piers," she said. "Find them, see if they're willing to try getting out of this nightmare, with us."

I could see Felicity standing at the bedroom window, upstairs in the zoo's big old brick building, watching us down here.

"And what if Caleb was wrong about them?" I said. "Or—or what if they're not there?"

"Then we try doing this on our own." Rachel unlocked the gate, I went out and she locked it after me.

She smiled, the bars between us. "They'll be there, just as Caleb said; he was a good guy."

"He still is."

I turned and left my friends behind. Rachel yelled out, "Be careful!"

I headed out alone. Me and these streets. Eighteen days since the attack, eighteen days of avoiding death at the hands of the infected. I walked through the park. Rocks shifted in rubble underfoot and rats scurried from a dead body. How I hated this place.

2

oday had started out freezing and damp, and now a wall of wet snowdrift blew hard against me in a headwind. I headed southeast, under the heavy, gray February sky, with the wind blowing around me and frozen rain falling. I'd learned to feel this weather now. When heavy snow rolls in, darkness comes early, time gets lost. In the streets it was easy to be lulled into a false sense of security, deaf and blind to what might lurk in the silence and shadows. How would this day end? Would it be any different from the others?

To catch my breath, I took shelter in an alcove, not that different from one in which I'd sheltered from similar weather, with a girl. We'd kissed. Anna. My first kiss, right here in this city, from a girl I would never see again, sharing an act full of heat and stomach-turning butterflies I might never know again. She'd tasted of strawberries. I smiled at that memory, licked my cracked lips. I could almost taste it.

Like so many, Anna never got to go home. She was one of the first to be taken in this attack. At least it was quick. I had no idea if she was religious or not, but I hoped there was someplace for her to go, someplace warm and sunny . . . The best I could offer was to remember her and others when I got home to Australia. When I got back. It seemed an impossible distance to travel.

The sun peeked out from behind the heavy winter clouds and illuminated the road that stretched out before me. Near the Hudson River I turned south, following streets I'd not walked before near the western edge of Manhattan. I liked the new sights here—desolate, sure, but this was an exploration of the unknown I felt I could handle. It was as if there was someone contriving to send me there, calling me onwards to the south.

After two blocks of weaving through smashed cars and downed buildings the road became impassable. Even so, this morning I felt driven. I trekked these streets with purpose. This wasn't some false hope, some blind excursion: I was looking for a group of *survivors,* even though the only evidence of their existence was what Caleb had told me.

If the group he'd told me about was still at Chelsea Piers, then I was relying on my ability to persuade them to leave. I hoped. I'd seen more of human nature in these past two weeks than I had in all my sixteen years; the best of it, and the worst. Was I crazy to expect anything of anyone, that as survivors we shared a common goal? It was my job to convince them, right? I'd *persuade* them it was safer to leave the city, that we *had* to get out. I'd take them via the zoo to get Rachel and Felicity and we could head north.

Then I saw something new. At the crossroads before me were three bodies, slumped on the packed snow, but not covered by it. They were fresh: there were traces of color in their cheeks and the blood on their flesh was thin and red, not black and congealed. Anyone could have seen they were not Chasers, and I didn't think they were the Chasers' victims—the work was too clean.

I'd known there must have been people who'd survived the attack. I just hadn't seen them. In true New Yorker fashion, perhaps they'd taken the advice given after 9/11 and barricaded themselves inside. Doors sealed up, windows shuttered, cupboards stocked with all kinds of long-life food. *Shelter in place.* That was my theory, anyway. But could anyone live that way for long? Maybe here was the answer. These people had had enough: they'd had to break free, to escape, to look for people like me, a way out. Only they hadn't made it. Had anyone noticed they were missing—and would they be missed now that they were . . . gone?

I tried not to think of this unknown. In fact, I sped up, as if there were people expecting me, waiting anxiously for my safe arrival.

But I didn't get far. Moments later, I stopped cold. A noise, feet crunching against snow; fast, like many pairs involved in a chase. I listened and looked—nothing. Sound carried by the wind? Shifting rubble cascading nearby? This deserted city was trying to spook me—

No. My fears were real.

Chasers.

I hid in an overturned school bus. Both the front windshield and rear window were in place but there was a black jagged hole of torn steel where the door had been. Dark, deep snow banked up against the side windows, which were almost at ground level.

There was a tear across the palm of my glove, and I knew I'd cut my hand badly—hands that had already taken such a battering. I couldn't see the wound but through my clenched fist I felt the warm, sticky blood. I was scared to breathe, my every motion loud and amplified in here. Through the grimy windshield I watched their feet shuffle as they passed.

The wind, blowing hard from the south, might keep the horizon's heavy storm away—maybe it would even skip Manhattan altogether. When it looked safe, I dropped down from the bus to the road and tore up a spare T-shirt to use as a bandage. I should have packed a medical kit. I tightened the straps of my backpack and continued south.

At the next intersection the breeze whipped past the corner building and carried with it smoke, the smell of burning gasoline and plastics. I covered my nose and mouth with the front of my sweatshirt, and ran across the intersection and down the next two blocks, before I cracked and took in heaving lungfuls of air. It tasted cold and sharp and clear, dizzying. *Gotta keep moving. Gotta get there, get off these streets.*

The unknown was getting to me. The familiar parts of Midtown in which I felt so safe now seemed so distant. Sure, I was headed towards something that stirred hope in my gut, but *getting* there . . .

At each intersection I stopped to check that the coast was clear before crossing the open terrain. I always stayed a few paces away from the dark facades of the storefronts, in case a Chaser jumped out and surprised me. I made sure my footing was on firm ground.

Gunfire crackled from the east. A few single shots, then a continuous burst of machine-gun fire. I recognized it immediately, even though before I arrived in New York I wouldn't have known the difference between the sound of an assault rifle and a pistol. I had never held a weapon, couldn't imagine depending on one for my basic protection. But now the need to survive had made me an expert. An image of last night flashed in my mind's eye: *the soldiers at their truck, shooting at the Chasers, the aircraft coming in on an attack run . . .*

The gunfire petered out and my awareness of the present returned. *Keep moving.*

I headed west at 56th. I knew I hadn't traveled along here before, but it reminded me of so many other streets: the widespread destruction had rendered mismatched city streets uniformly gray and cold and frozen. Manhattan was one big canvas of repeating patterns. I passed a mail truck: which reminded of when I met Caleb. I checked inside it— nothing, no living thing. Nothing but windswept snowdrift and ash.

At the next intersection, my back to a wall, I watched for movement reflected in a cracked pane of a store window. It seemed clear but then something shifted in the shadows across the street.

People? More survivors, trying to make sense of what made no sense at all? How would they react on seeing me? What if I didn't have the answers they wanted to hear?

I could see them more clearly now. They were Chasers, but I could tell that they were only very recently turned, and had not yet had to fight, to kill. They were dressed in their warmest, best clothes. These were people who were used to taking care of themselves, who had never had to be content with making do. But that didn't stop them looking wild. Angry. I smiled, tentatively, for a moment, as they emerged from the shadows. *I've outrun you before . . .* As I feared, they were anything but pleased to see me. These were the *chasing* kind; demented, driven crazy by isolation and captivity.

Flat out, I ran down Seventh Avenue, the six of them after me. Seemed the chase was new to them; they strove to use muscles that had been inactive for over two weeks. The effort and pain intensified their rage. Their hunger drove them on, relentless.

My feet skidded out as I turned onto 44th Street, falling as I slid on the ice and tripped over a street sign that was bent across the sidewalk and concealed by snow. *Run!* Got up and ran. Stopped at Ninth Avenue, looked back—they were *gaining!*

South—keep moving south. I ran as fast as I could, my arms and legs pumping, my feet slipping and sliding over uneven ground and ice. At the end of this block I turned left, looked back—couldn't see them yet . . .

Then they appeared. Maybe it was the distance or my imagination, but they didn't look exhausted: they just kept coming for me.

I backed away, my feet heavy lumps of concrete. I turned and ran.

At the next corner, at Tenth Avenue, there was a tall building about fifty stories high, an ugly seventies thing that stuck out in this neighborhood. I headed for it.

The awning said "West Bank" and something about a theatre. I passed a café, doubled back, ran inside. I stayed low, tried to lock the door but there was only a keyed lock—I backed into the café, stopped dead still.

There was someone behind me. A presence . . .

A cough. Deep, like it belonged to a big man.

I didn't want to turn around—*If this is how I am going to go, let it be quick.*

3

My hand found the Glock pistol in my pocket. I drew it out, turned around—

The big guy was standing maybe five paces away. He was in his twenties, massive in every proportion—comic-book big, like that rock guy from *Fantastic Four* or *Hellboy* or *The Hulk*. (I'd read a lot of comics during my short time with Caleb.) He had shaved dark hair and a tattoo that snaked up through his collar, around his neck. Another guy emerged through swinging doors from the kitchen. He was my height and size, but older, mid-thirties maybe, ghostly pale and not much hair up top.

The three of us got the measure of each other. Both of them saw the pistol and something registered. By that recognition, I knew that they weren't Chasers.

"Hey," the big guy said, eating a chocolate bar. "Nice piece."

I looked down at my pistol but kept it out. I checked behind me, out the frosty windows, and saw the movement of the Chasers nearing.

"I'm being followed," I said. "We need to hide."

"Hide?" the big guy said, unfazed. "What for?"

"To avoid being killed," I said, my voice quiet. "We need to move, and quick."

"Who is it?" he asked.

"Chasers," I whispered. He looked at me weirdly. I pointed behind me. "The infected—the bad kind, a group of them."

The older one, a friendly face behind a neat beard, said, "Quick, follow me."

A moment later the three of us stood silent in the kitchen. A tiny round window in one of the double swinging doors provided a view out to the restaurant.

"How many?" the big guy asked, as if he was considering the odds if it came to a confrontation. I recognized in what he said and how he said it that they were survivors, like me.

"Shh!" the older guy said. He was close to the kitchen doors, peering out the little window.

We heard a chair being bumped in the restaurant.

There seemed to be no other way out of this kitchen; in any case, I was too tense to move. I swallowed hard, the pistol shaking in my good hand, blood dripping from my wounded one. Could the Chasers smell it, the blood? I put my tight fist into the pocket of my bulky FDNY fireman's coat.

The big guy produced what I expected to be a gun but turned out to be a little digital video camera. He started filming. There was something about that act that settled me, as if it took some of the danger out of the situation. "For perpetuity," he whispered to me. "All this—it's history in the making. I'm recording as much of it as I can."

The guy by the doors stood still and watched the restaurant. I inched towards him as quietly as I could, but my wet shoes made tiny squeegee sounds against the floor. I cringed with each move-induced sound, then took up a position where I could look through the gap between the swinging doors. We stayed hidden to be sure the coast remained clear, none of us daring to make a sound.

A Chaser stood at the front of the restaurant, half in and half out the front door, his back to us; an ordinary-enough-looking guy, if it weren't for the dried blood around his mouth. His buddies were outside. I could make out five of them, men, maybe a woman too, all as alert and searching as him, waiting. My hand squeezed the pistol's grip.

Just as I thought he was leaving—

There was a noise, behind me—the big guy had bumped against an oven.

The Chaser turned, looking around at the empty tables and chairs between us. My gloved hand sweated around the pistol's grip. The Chaser was still, listening, smelling at the air—or maybe I imagined that. *If it came to it, I could do it.* I'd done it once. My mouth was dry and I felt like bursting out of the kitchen and taking him by surprise.

He glanced around, a final accusatory glare—then he bolted, the door slamming closed in his wake, and

I could see him and his cohorts running off down the road the way they'd come.

"Okay, they're gone," the older guy said, still by the doors; he let out a deep breath, then turned to me, offered his hand. "I'm Daniel."

"Jesse," I said, shaking his hand.

"Don't shoot us," he said with a smile.

I looked down at the pistol, the familiar unwelcome weight that could so easily carry with it a list of demands.

"Yeah, that was intense," I said, reaching back and tucking it into the side pocket of my pack.

"Name's Bob." The guy with the shaved head, Bob, shook my hand; he filmed the exchange.

"You guys here getting supplies?" I asked, gesturing to some crates of canned and packaged food.

"Yep," Daniel replied. "You?"

"I'm on my way to—" Then I thought better of it. Play it cool, I decided. "Just passing through." I knew it sounded weak, and it clearly wasn't enough to satisfy.

"Where have you been based since the attack?"

"Midtown, near Rockefeller Center," I said. "Is all that food just for the two of you?"

"There's about forty of us," Daniel said.

"Forty?"

"And counting," Bob added. "Seems to grow by the day, and I usually get the short straw to be sent out on foraging trips."

"What about you?" Daniel asked.

"Just me," I said. His eyes searched mine and I looked to the floor. I didn't want to tell these two guys about Rachel and Felicity, not yet. Bob kept the camera rolling and as I felt myself holding back from these guys its beady eye began to make me feel self-conscious. "I'm out here alone, aren't I?"

"Well," Bob said, his face softened by a big grin, "you're not alone anymore, little buddy."

Daniel clarified: "What he means, Jesse, is that you're welcome to come by and see our setup: have something to eat, stay around if you like it."

Bob added, "It's safe, and got everything you'd want or need."

"Up to you."

"Thanks, guys," I said, stalling. At that moment I was thinking of Caleb—the way he'd encouraged me to spend more time with him, not to race back to Rachel and the animals, and I'd *listened* to him, and . . . well, I made a good friend as a result, sure, but I'd lost time and we'd wasted . . . ah, hell.

"Well, can't hang around here forever," Daniel said, hefting a crate off a bench. "Bob, let's get this stuff home." Big plastic bins of food that they'd ransacked from this place were packed and ready to go, a good several hundred pounds' worth.

"How are you getting that back?" I asked.

"Pickup out front," Daniel replied. "Bob, load the rest of those wine boxes, too."

"On it," Bob said. He was a hulk of a man but obe-

dient to Daniel like a smart dog, or a UFC heavy-
weight on a tight leash. He handled those bins and
boxes more easily than I could heft a bucket of water.

"Here, I'll help you," I said, realizing I was reluc-
tant to let go of these guys completely. I'd let Caleb
go, just like Anna, Mini, and Dave, the friends I'd
kept alive in my imagination for the first dozen days.
I'd known them in life for only a couple of weeks, but
when I saw them dead I decided to carry on with the
living images in my head. I tried to do that with
Caleb, but all I could see was his bloody mouth as he
hovered over a dead or dying soldier.

Had I lost Felicity and Rachel by leaving them at
the zoo? Was it worth risking more loss by making
new friends now? And why these people? Who knew
who else would turn up on my way to Chelsea Piers?
Maybe there were pockets of *good* survivors somewhere, groups who'd managed to hold it together,
who were frightened but dealing with it.

Daniel led the way outside. He took his time looking around and checking that the coast was clear
before motioning us out. We loaded the bed of a massive double-cab Ford pickup, more like a truck than
the pickups I'd known back home.

Bob let his camera hang from the lanyard around
his neck. We grabbed a side of a bin each, and carried
it out, while Daniel held open the doors. Then the
three of us shuttled out the remaining boxes and bags.
It was windy now, the strong northeasterly was back
and with it came the weather. By the time we'd se-

cured the transit and were locked inside, the storm hit in force. Heavy rain, cold enough for snow but too torrential to form ice.

Daniel started the engine, put the heater and A/C on to de-mist. It smelled like old wet socks and bad breath in here. The outside temp read thirty degrees Fahrenheit. The biting wind had made it feel at least twenty degrees colder than that. My teeth were chattering. Bob caught it all on camera.

"Can we drop you someplace near?" Daniel asked.

I made myself think of Caleb again. I owed it to him to go to Chelsea Piers, to seek these people out. And then to return to Rachel and Felicity with answers. Besides, what choice did I have while this storm lasted?

"Um—" I checked my watch.

"You gotta be somewhere?" Bob asked. "Someplace else?"

"Just seeing how far off nightfall is," I said. It was still a few hours away—the sun set around 5 P.M., which always seemed far earlier than the winters back home. I doubted very much if I could make it all the way to the piers before nightfall, not in this weather, and I couldn't risk being on the streets—wouldn't hear or see a Chaser until it was too late . . . "Where are you guys staying?"

Daniel said, "Chelsea Piers."

"Sorry?"

"It's down along the Hudson," Daniel explained. "South of here."

I had to be sure I heard right: "You said *Chelsea Piers*?"

"Yes."

"You all right?" Bob asked me.

"Yeah, cool, it's just—" My head was spinning. I let out a sigh. Was this a happy coincidence, or just more dismal proof that this city was largely deserted—that maybe these guys and their group were the only normal people left?

"Yeah, the Chelsea Piers, in the sports complex— though not for too much longer, I hope," Daniel said. I smiled at that: *Caleb had been right!*

"If you want to come with us, let us know now, or I can drop you away from here far as we can on our way. Like I said, up to you."

"I'll come, sure," I said. "Thanks."

"Cool," Bob said, putting his hand up for me to high-five, filming that too. "Most of the people there are decent."

"Most?" I said, barely able to hear him and be heard over the din on the truck's metal roof.

Daniel did a U-turn and headed south. He drove well, like he was familiar with the route, comfortable with the conditions. I studied the back of Bob's massive head as he filmed the streetscape. A few scars were visible, pale lines against dark stubble. I told myself not to judge by outward appearances. I remembered seeing some gang members on the subway and how the other passengers had given them a wide berth. Ultimately, they weren't so different from each other; they'd all died in this attack, died just like so many others.

I smiled as I rode in the car. Here I was with other *survivors*! I'd found them, and it felt as though this was meant to be. And, as they'd offered me so much without me giving anything in return, I decided to tell them about Felicity and Rachel—and about Caleb. It seemed like the least I could do.

4

It was a twenty-minute drive, zigzagging and squeez-ing through the gridlock of wrecked vehicles, winding around downed buildings and avoiding craters big enough to swallow the vehicle whole.

They remembered Caleb. How he'd passed through one day, a nonchalant air about him. He'd stayed for a meal and exchanged information, then he'd left.

"I felt sorry for him," Bob said. "Caleb, he seemed like a good guy."

"Why's that?" I asked.

"Just the way Tom treated him—you'll meet Tom soon enough."

"Treated him? Like how?"

"Just a difference of opinion, I guess," Bob said. "He's not one to be challenged like that, and with Caleb getting people all excited by hopes of some way out of the city . . ."

This Tom guy sounded like a jerk. "Well, you can tell that guy that Caleb didn't get to see his way out of this city."

Bob looked to Daniel, as if unsure who would ask the delicate question—if they needed to know at all. Maybe it was safer not to get too familiar?

"You talk like he's gone," Bob said.

"Did I?" I asked, a little worried. "Really?"

"Seems that way," Daniel said, his voice soothing away doubt and reluctance. "What happened?"

I explained about the explosion that had turned Caleb into a Chaser. First, I told them about the un-exploded missiles. I'd seen one on my first day, and Caleb had reported one in an abandoned property. Then Starkey—whoever he was; would I ever truly know?—the only adult in his group who'd bothered to talk to me seriously, had warned me of the missile in the back of the military truck. *"When it explodes,"* he'd said, *"it will release the biological agent, you understand?"* The agent that turned people into Chasers. I'd run as he'd instructed me, but Caleb was still dragging bodies to safety when the explosion happened. *KLAPBOOM!* For a moment, Caleb was lost to me in the smoke and fireball and when I saw him again, it had happened. There was Caleb: at the body of a dead soldier. Drinking him.

They hadn't interrupted, but Bob couldn't hold back his questions. "This guy—Starkey—he was part of the US military?"

"I'm not sure," I said. "Their trucks had USAM-RIID stenciled on them. That's a scientist outfit, I think." I remembered the words Felicity had used, drawing on knowledge gained from her brother. "They specialize in virology and combating biological warfare."

Daniel nodded. "Stands for US Army Medical Research Institute of Infectious Diseases."

"So what were they doing with the missile in the back of the truck?" asked Bob.

"I'd thought that they could have been taking it for tests," I said.

"Could have been covering up evidence," Bob added. "Biological warfare, you know." Then he said, "Why—?" his question hung in the air, rhetorical. "Why all that, then have an aircraft of our own come in and hit them?"

I shrugged. "What I do know is that that's how you become one of the chasing kind of infected, like those we encountered back there: *proximity* to the explosion."

These guys were hungry for information, and hung on my every word. Sharing news can bring you closer to the person doing the listening. I could see their empathy grow and, with it, mine did too. I wished I had more to tell, more to share, but this was enough for now. Besides, I felt tired being in this hot cab of the truck, and then . . .

Chelsea Piers.

Chelsea Piers was a long, bleak, industrial facade of corrugated iron running along the Hudson River side of Eleventh Avenue. We pulled up to the southern-most end, at some kind of sports center at the corner of West 18th—golf, mainly, by the look of the advertising outside. I could see that the pier had a massive ten-story-high net along the three sides to stop golf balls from flying into the Hudson—the scale of this place made it feel safe. I liked that it looked deserted: there was nothing from the outside that signaled there was a group of over forty survivors living inside.

"Bob," Daniel said, and it was all he needed to say: Bob jumped out of the cab. Cold, hard wind stabbed into the cabin in those couple of seconds the passenger door was open. I watched him run over to a big roller door and bang on it three times. I felt Daniel's eyes in the rearview mirror, and I looked out my window. On the other side of the street was a big building of curved, white frosted glass, almost invisible in this weather; it looked safe and solid, the kind of place one could easily retreat to.

"Jesse, are you okay?" Daniel asked.

"Yeah," I said.

"You'll be fine. But I think it's best if you don't tell the others about what happened to Caleb just yet. It'll . . . spook them."

"Yeah, okay," I said. It seemed reasonable enough, since that news carried a weighty fear: *Be wary of being out in the streets, for, if your luck's run out, you just might become a Chaser, one of the damned . . .*

Bob waved us through the open roller door. Daniel drove forward, pulling the monster vehicle inside the base of the complex. We got out as the big steel door slammed shut behind us.

Inside the receiving bay, by the glow of the headlights and some handheld flashlights, I could make out a group of people headed towards us: about a dozen women and men who quickly made short work of lugging in the gear. Everyone greeted me in passing.

Practically everyone wore evidence of survival: some had their arms in casts, another couple limped past on crutches. No one's face was unblemished by a bruise or scar. I imagined how misplaced Caleb must have looked, sailing in on his gleaming motorbike, looking young and fit, maybe even confident. Of course, I knew what was on the inside, but had they seen that?

"Hi."

"Hello."

"Hi."

Despite all that had gone on in this city, inside these words was a little piece of normality, of people making the best of being survivors. As I watched them shuttling about, stowing the gear we'd brought, it pricked the hairs on the back of my neck in a good way. Just like sharing information with Bob and Daniel, this sight—of survivors so happy to see me and to see a fresh batch of supplies—made me wish I had *more* to give. There was a girl about my age, maybe a bit older; I almost tripped because I was looking at her while trying to lug in a bin of food with Bob handling the other side.

"Hey, watch it, little buddy," Bob said.

"Sorry."

He grinned, catching me looking back at her.

"What?"

"Nothin'." He was still all smiles and I felt my face flush red. "Yep, there's still girls around."

I was embarrassed. "I know."

"She's nice."

"Shut up."

He laughed. "Ah, to be a teenager again. Better you than me."

We dumped the food down in a hall full of supplies, where a couple of people inventoried and sorted the new stock. It was warm and dry in here, so different from the building back at the zoo where Rachel and Felicity would be hunkering down to weather this storm.

"Come on, I'll show you around," Bob said.

Up a level, there were chairs and couches scattered throughout a reception area, people lounging and resting, talking and listening, reading and playing cards. Their enjoyment was infectious. A group of kids ran about, playing some kind of tag game. Carried on the breeze of an open door out onto an AstroTurfed pier-turned-golf-driving-range was the heady smell of a barbecue, which made my stomach groan and my mouth salivate.

Around a corner behind a screen were a couple of people lying on makeshift gurneys: closer, I could see that they were patched up with bandages but they didn't seem too badly off. Bob noticed a drop of blood fall from my gloved hand as I put it into my pocket. Even though I was among many wounded, I didn't want to signal the weaknesses that could overcome me at any minute. I was alone, after all, just one person who maybe would need to act with the strength of many to persuade them to part from their safety net. The safest way to get home was to head north—because the contagion was worse in the warmer climes—and be among as large a group as possible. We couldn't wait for more attacks and for the Chasers to become more ruthless.

"We've got a doctor here," Bob said. "I think he should take a look at that hand."

"Surgeon, actually," a tall, tanned man said. He was fifty or so, taut leathery skin with an orange-ish tan, thick black hair brushed just so. "I'm Tom."

"Jesse," I said. I noticed that the pretty girl I'd seen in the receiving bay was watching me from across the room, talking to three younger kids. She was shorter than me, and had sandy-brown hair in a ponytail. Cheerleader kind of pretty.

Tom addressed me as he put on latex gloves and used scissors to cut my torn glove off.

"Sorry?" I asked, through gritted teeth as he poked and prodded.

"I asked you if you were planning on staying here."

"I, ah—"

"He's sheltering with us until the storm passes," said Daniel, falling in next to me. "Then he can decide what he wants to do."

"Your hand will be fine. It needs a cleanup and dressing; I'll have someone attend to it." He put a wad of gauze on my palm, then took off his gloves, and tossed them into a bin and moved on to the other patients.

"Don't mind him," Daniel said. "He likes to seem important—first impressions and all that."

I understood. "Yeah, that's cool."

"Come on," Daniel clapped a hand on my shoulder. "I'll introduce you to some friends."

He gestured to Bob, who was back to filming his documentary or whatever. I followed Daniel, who seemed to be headed for that girl, and I tried to do my best not to make a fool of myself. I remembered getting tongue-tied when I'd met Felicity, but surely that was the effect of finally meeting her after days of longing for her company, right?

What was so special about this girl? She was pretty, sure, but I couldn't let myself be distracted by her. I had good reason to be here now, and I'd make sure they all soon knew that we had good reason to leave.

We approached the group of teens. One guy, thirteen maybe; a girl his age who was strikingly similar, and another who resembled the comic-book guy from *The Simpsons*.

"Paige, this is Jesse, our guest for the day," Daniel said. "Paige's father is Tom, who you just met."

It was her eyes that entranced me and it took me a few seconds of staring to figure out why: not just the perfectly shaped almonds, the long dark lashes: it was her irises. They were different colors, one brilliant blue, the other a dark green-brown.

"Oh, okay." *Damn.* Why did she have to be related to *him*? "Hi."

"Hey." Paige looked at me as if I was a novelty, some kind of new toy.

"Paige, could you show Jesse around, get him sorted out for lunch?"

"Sure," she said, a little too chirpy.

"Your father's getting someone to see to his hand."

"I can do that," she replied, all smiles.

Daniel clapped my shoulder again, and left for the terrace looking over the pier into the murky Hudson River. Bob stayed behind, filming me, Paige and the others nearby. He crouched a little and slowly panned around in a tracking close-up.

"Bob, you can stop that now," Paige said. He did as he was told and went in search of something else to document.

Paige produced a medical kit and opened it on the table. "We'll get you cleaned up," she said, her chair facing mine, taking my hand in hers.

"Okay," I said.

Paige's hands were small, soft but cold. She was

well-tanned compared to others here but a similar tone to me—it was summer back home in Australia. I flinched when she touched me, her fingers on my hands and wrists, ticklish, electric, real.

"Hurts?"

"A little," I said. I felt my cheeks blush. I tried thinking of cricket. "Where are you from?"

"L.A.," she replied. She washed my hands with a damp cloth, using sterilized water from a plastic medical squeeze bottle, cleaning out the grazes, reopening the deep cut on my palm. I couldn't stop looking at her face, her skin, her eyes. Every now and then she'd connect with an exposed nerve ending and I'd cringe.

"Might sting," she said, spraying disinfectant on my hands.

"Ouch." It hurt but I was glad—it took my mind away from her smile.

She stuck some bandages on the heels of my palms, which I'd grazed raw. She wrapped the hand that was still leaking blood in a tight padded bandage.

"Job done."

"Thanks," I said.

"Feel okay?"

"It's great," I said. My hands were painful, but they rested gently in her lap, held by her own, as she looked into my eyes. Her expression was full of doubt. Not her own, I realized, but a reflection of mine.

"What is it?"

"It's—nothing," I said.

In leggings and a tight sweater, Paige's look and manner reminded me of a couple of the popular, untouchable chicks back at school, the ones who always seemed way out of my league; but here she was, here we were, talking. I decided not to look at her body anymore. As we got up and made our way through the room I tried to keep next to her, in stride, and said "Hi" to at least a dozen people she introduced me to.

"Hope my dad was nice to you."

"Yeah," I said.

"It's just he's so busy, running around treating everyone who passes through here," she explained. "He's, like . . . *frustrated* I guess—like all of us, yeah?"

"Yeah."

"You wanna put your pack over there?" she asked, pointing to the doors that led to the terrace.

"Okay," I said. I put my pack down next to some others, hung my FDNY coat over it, looked at the Glock pistol's handle hanging out the side pocket. I reached for it—

Her tanned hand touched my arm as if to hold me back. "You won't need that here," she said. "We're safe here. If that's what you're worried about."

"Oh, no, it's cool. I'm just—"

"You're just—what?"

In that moment, I'd lost any ground I'd gained between us. How could I bring up what I needed to say? *I just want to know if you guys will leave with me— as a group, safety in numbers and all that.*

"Hungry?"

I smiled, saved from the moment. Be patient. *Get to know them.* "Yeah, starved."

"Come on then," she said, reaching out to lead me by my good hand. "I'll show you where the food's at."

5

I don't know why I hesitated to leave the gun behind—we were safe behind these walls, with all these people, right? I nodded, and took the pistol out, ejected the magazine, pulled back the slide so that the round in the chamber popped out. I tucked the empty pistol deep into the backpack's side pocket, zipped it up tight, then pocketed the ammo.

"I just thought—I mean, there's kids around," I said, "and I'm used to always having it loaded and—"

"It's cool," she said, smiling. "Come on, let's get you fed." I followed Paige down the walkway, into a putting green where the barbecue was set up. There were a couple of guys cooking away—they had piles of the cooked meats I'd smelled stacked up on a table, while others served people with scoops of pasta salad and tinned vegetables. There were literally hundreds of condiments on another table, where people queued and helped themselves to pickles and sauces and sauerkraut; another table had stacks of cups and giant steaming urns labeled COFFEE, TEA, COCOA. People sat around in little groups, chatting and eating, a constant hum of conversation.

"What is it?" Paige asked.

I looked across at her, realizing I'd just been standing there inside the doorway, watching, my mouth hanging open like I was catching flies.

"I . . . I've kinda dreamed about coming across a place like this."

"Like this?"

"A refuge, full of life," I said. "I haven't seen so many people like this, not for ages. And they're all— they all seem, so—"

"Normal?"

I nodded.

"That's a cycle on a washing machine."

I smiled.

"Normal. It's a cycle—"

"Right, got it," I said, following her inside.

"I so understand if you want to sit on your own," she said. "If you're a bit shell-shocked by all this."

"No, not at all," I said as we approached a table. On the way in we collected a plateful of food each. We sat down next to a woman whose ears were wadded with gauze, with a bandage wrapped around her head like a headband. It reminded me of bodies I'd seen, of people who'd bled from the ears and eyes, as if the concussive force of the explosions had expanded inside their heads. I'd seen a lot of things that I never wanted to be reminded of.

"Jesse, this is my stepmom, Audrey," Paige said.

Audrey smiled at me. She was pretty, far too nice-looking to be with Tom. Paige wrote something on a little spiral-bound pad and Audrey read it and looked at me and said: "Hi Jesse."

She put out her hand and I shook it. It was soft and warm. She looked at my bandaged hand, where the blood had soaked through, with concern.

"Drink?" an older lady asked me. She stood by our table, with a tub of little juice boxes.

"Thanks," I said, taking an apple juice. Paige took one too. The old lady winked at me as she left.

I ate a piece of steak with some fried onions and tomato sauce, a big slice of fresh warm bread on the side.

"Have you not eaten in a while?" Paige asked.

"I have, but . . . it's—I was going to say, 'it's a long story,' but I guess it's just that I'm hungry and exhausted today," I said through a mouthful, then I made myself slow down. I tried to eat with more decorum, to give a better impression—but then I bit the inside of my cheek. I hid my pain with a drink of juice and tried to smile.

"Where have you been living?" Paige asked, reading off her stepmother's pad. Pity, I'd have liked her to ask such a question of me of her own accord.

"30 Rock, mainly," I said, eating some pasta salad. Oh man, this food was good—plenty of basil pesto, cheese, and olives. I added some dried chili flakes.

"30 Rock—as in the TV show?"

"Um, I guess that's where they set it—there's a

TV studio in there," I said. "It's the GE Building, at 30 Rockefeller Plaza. Big and safe, above the city. I stayed on the sixty-fifth floor, the Rainbow Room. Great view—and there's observation decks above that. Well, I mean the view wasn't *great*—but it's high, you can see a lot from up there."

"How does the city look?" Paige asked.

I put my fork down for a moment, and described the destruction I'd seen. She wrote all this down for Audrey. Audrey smiled, gave a little nod of approval, and said in a little, tired voice that clearly couldn't hear itself: "How—many—people—were—you—with?"

"None, there," I said, picking at my food now, pushing it around, my appetite disappearing as the memories rose inside me. "It was just me. I was on a subway when the attack happened—"

I told them my story. Not from the optimism of my initial airplane ride from Melbourne to New York, nor those first few exciting days of being in this bustling city, the introductions when I arrived at the UN leadership summer camp, making unlikely but cool friends, but from the moment of the attack—that moment when we all became the same, when we all could be labeled *survivors*. I told my story from when I emerged from the subway tunnel, to describing in more detail what I'd seen from 30 Rock.

Then I explained about Anna, Mini, and Dave. Of all the kids on the UN Ambassadors camp, the four of us had got along best. We'd become a good team. Although maybe we'd just spent a little too much time together, because the conversation on the subway as we headed for the 9/11 memorial was more fraught than usual.

But it was nothing compared to the panic when the subway car tilted and the lights flickered. A vast ball of fire chased the train and sent us crashing to the floor, awaiting the oblivion that came—first, darkness and pain, and then, a last exit for them. For me it began what was to be the delirium of my first twelve days of being alone. But I broke from my solitude— I had to. I had more than cherished the memory of those friends. I'd made them live on in my mind right up to the moment where I was at last able to accept that they were dead and that if I were to survive, I needed to rely solely on myself.

I waited for Paige's notes to catch up. The gentle rhythm of her writing, the faint scratching of pen on paper, put me at ease; as if it put a distance between me recalling and telling the events, reminding me not only of the importance of information, but of sharing in whatever humanity might be left.

"That's so awesome of you," Paige said. "I mean, there's no way I could have survived all that on my own, like no way."

I told them about Rachel and Felicity at the zoo. I suspected that Bob and Daniel would filter the story of Caleb's transformation when they felt it was time. I'd told *my* story, and it took the rest of my meal and a half block of chocolate, while Paige sat there and ate the other half. Her stepmother had two cups of tea and twenty new pages of closely written words in her notebook. I'd thought it was hard enough being a survivor without means of communication, and not knowing what had happened and who did all this: imagine being in her situation, wholly dependent on others to hear for her.

Audrey had tears in her eyes when I told her and Paige that I had to let Mini, Anna, and Dave go, on my way to the 79th Street Boat Basin. Especially Anna . . .

"Because . . . they would have held you back?"

"Yeah, that's right." I nodded, wondering if I sounded totally nuts to the point where Paige's dad might try to put me in a straitjacket. "They'd kept me sane—well, if you could call it that. They kept me company during my time at 30 Rock, through the briefest of glimpses and conversations. Then, when I was being chased, I knew I could survive out there alone, and I was right: letting them go helped bring me here, right?"

"You must miss them."

"I—yeah, I do. But mainly I regret that I couldn't do anything to save them."

Audrey cried, then Paige put an arm around her shoulders. A single tear fell from her blue eye and several more were held there, on her long eyelashes. I blinked away some tears of my own, and let out a funny noise, part whimper, part embarrassed cough.

"I'm sorry," Paige said, reading from the pad those two words that her stepmother had written, and since we'd bonded over this, since it had been such an intimate session of storytelling, we all felt it hit home.

6

Sensing that Paige and her stepmother needed to be alone to reflect on the people they'd loved and lost, to say nothing of the new facts I'd burdened them with, I headed up to the top level of the complex.

Everyone in this place had work to do; they'd settled in for the long haul. They had formed into groups, little cells designed to accomplish tasks or else just to hang around with, seek companionship and consolation. Each had their delegated tasks down pat, and I felt pretty useless being the new kid on the block. People seemed content—happy even—doing their jobs. Did I want to feel that, as long as I was here? Doing something each day to merely survive? Hadn't I had enough of all that? Even back in the pre-attack world, I knew that, no matter what, when I finished high school I was not going to embark on a career where I "lived to work" like that. I mean, where was the freedom, the choice, in such an existence? If I was going to do such work *all* day, *every*

day, I'd much rather do it back at the Central Park
Zoo with Rachel and Felicity. They had more on
their plate than merely seeing out each new day; they
had many mouths to feed, living creatures that needed
their help, a purpose that transcended selfishness.

Bob was up on the roof, doing a final security
sweep of the area while the sun was still up. The smell
of smoke and ash hung in the wet air. Dark water
swirled and eddied in the Hudson. A few overturned
hulls of broken boats floated about. Across on the
street side there were good views up and down
Eleventh Avenue: smashed and burned-out wrecks of
vehicles were dotted all the way up and down it,
blotches against the white-gray streetscape.

"Looks like a war zone, doesn't it?" said Bob.

"It is," I said.

"Yeah. And once again, this is the front line."

"Once again?"

"Like 9/11," he said. His words hung there for a
while. "All this out here reminds me of some pictures
I saw in a book about the first US–Iraq war. Some
highway in the desert, littered with thousands of destroyed vehicles, all burned-out wrecks melted into
the road and sand."

He scanned the darkening streets with his small
binoculars.

"Have they ever attacked here? The infected, I
mean."

He looked at me. He had a face that could go real
hard real quick.

"The infected—*Chasers* you called them earlier to-day, right?"

I nodded.

"No." He shook his head. "But we've been hit twice, by people."

"People?"

"Shootin' at us, at first, and then, the second time, a group of guys drove by and firebombed the store-front down there. Sons of bitches even landed one up on the roof here. Look."

He pointed to scorch marks on the concrete roof; an area the size of a tennis court was blackened and charred and it seemed the snow no longer liked to settle there.

"What people?"

"Survivors like us. Last week."

"Shit!" I said, thinking about all the families down-stairs, all those survivors, being attacked by their own. I thought about those fresh corpses I'd seen lying on the snow—victims of their need to escape. And I thought about who might have attacked them. There are always people who'll exploit a situation, no mat-ter how desperate life is, even if it means turning on the only other people they might rely upon. Maybe they're thinking that when there's no civilization to be a part of, what's the point in being civilized? We're all killers, potentially; it's inescapable, an instinct that will consume you if you're not careful.

Time was running out. I had to get out of this city. So why was I hesitant about asking him if he'd leave here with me and any other survivors who wanted to tag along? It just didn't feel right to blurt straight into it. I realized that although we'd shared stories, I still knew very little about him.

So I asked, "You live in New York?"

"Only for a bit."

"Tourist?"

"Nah. I'm more of a drifter, never spend too long in one place," he said, kicking some snow off the edge of the roof. "Bit of work for the military, bit of work in prisons, couple of rigs out in the Gulf, always someplace different. Worked here way back, returned a few weeks ago."

He took out a small bottle of bourbon, unscrewed the top, took a swig and passed it to me. I had a small sip; it tasted like bitter fire, made me cough.

"Never really put down any roots, you know? You could say I had nothing to lose when all this happened, but it doesn't make it any easier to take."

"Yeah . . ." I took the binoculars, looked at the opposite shoreline. "Any family around here?"

He shook his head. "Nope. Just a few friends and, like I said, I was passing through—was gonna bug out once I'd put a bit more money in the bank."

"Shit happens, huh?"

"Sure does, little buddy," he said, his expression wistful as he scanned out across the Hudson. His alert eyes took in everything. "Sure does."

We walked the perimeter of the roof. We talked about the weather and what it'd be like elsewhere.

"How come there are no boats here at the piers?"
I asked.

"We figure that those who got here first, immediately after the attack, bugged out on those that were still seaworthy."

It seemed a reasonable answer and reflected what I imagined went on at the 79th Street Boat Basin. I trudged across to the northern side of the snow-covered roof. I pointed up Eleventh, passed him the binoculars, and he checked out a group of Chasers headed south.

"That kind? They hunt at twilight and into the night," he said. "They're smart. Probably smarter than us."

I shivered at the thought.

"Bob, I've got to ask you something," I said, the moment as good as any: "What would it take for you to try and leave this city?"

"A new dawn," he said. "Leave here? I'd give it a try in a heartbeat. Wouldn't want to leave any of these folks behind, though."

"Oh."

"Look, your friend Caleb?"

I nodded.

"When he came here, he got people all amped up about a route clear out of the city."

"Which route?" I asked, already knowing the answer—it was something *I'd* told Caleb during our first proper discussion.

"He said there was some road clear to the north,"

Bob said, glassing the streets again. "Thing was, it got a few guys so excited by the prospect, they said they'd go out and give it a look-see."

"And?"

He looked at me.

"Next day, I was out, just six blocks north of here, for supplies; found them, the four of them, dead."

I felt sick.

"How—how'd they die?"

"Gunshot wounds, but the infected had got to them too; had to chase a couple off their carcasses."

I did that. *I'd* told Caleb, Caleb told them, I was responsible for their deaths . . . No, not for their deaths. Crazy people killed them. But it was my news that had put them in harm's way.

"Ain't nothin' to be done about it," Bob said. "They were grown men, bigger than you. They knew the risks, and they made that choice themselves."

I nodded.

"Does everyone here know?"

He nodded.

"And now they're too spooked to leave?"

"Give it time, they'll all come around."

Give it time?

"Bob, we might not—what if we don't have time?"

We passed the charred section of roof on our way to the steel stairs heading down.

"Don't need to convince me of that."

7

Bob's revelations made me sick in my stomach. If they were not going to move, then I was wasting time here. First light, I could leave, back to the zoo, take my chances heading out with the girls—but if it was dangerous for four grown men to head north, what chance for a sixteen-year-old and a couple of girls barely older? Little to none.

But part of me thought that if I could convince anyone here, it might be Paige. She seemed to like me. Better yet, if I could convince her, get her on-board, that might bring on Audrey, then Tom, and with his reasoning might come the people who were too spooked to leave because of what had happened to those who'd dared venture out.

I found Paige playing poker with a few others. I made a beeline for her: she'd bathed and was wearing track clothes, pajamas maybe, her hair still wet and wrapped in a towel. I joined in and quickly bet myself out of the game. The same thing happened to Paige and, game over, I followed her out.

When I looked in on one of the groups, through the glass wall, I saw a middle-aged couple quietly arguing.

"Kinda surprises me," I said to Paige, settling on a new thought that had just hit me.

"What's that?"

"That, in there—the arguing. That there's still anger, there's still confusion, all that baggage between people."

"Baggage?" she said, looking back to the couple.

"Whatever it is we carry around. Guilt, regrets, anger, all that useless stuff getting in the way of living in the now and surviving."

Earlier on, all I'd seen was these people's cheerful acceptance of their situation. But there was division here. Maybe that was something I could use to get people to come with me. Leaving this city with half this group was a better prospect for me and Felicity and Rach than no one leaving but us.

All I had to go on was my few days of UN camp training before the attack. We'd sat in on talks and lectures about negotiating skills, delegation, and second-guessing the decision making of others. We'd participated in mock scenarios that made us confront what the facilitator called "the ugly reality of diplomacy." I'd never have guessed that, two weeks on, I'd be dealing with real-life situations fraught with all these issues and more. Would Paige or the others believe me that the risk involved in seeking out a better, safer existence was worth it?

I wanted to take her someplace quiet, but she led us to the adjoining room, an office now set up as a makeshift chapel. "I want you to see this," she said.

Paige and I watched as Daniel led about twenty people in prayer before bed. Bob entered and moved up front, a happy little preacher's boy inside the body of a pro wrestler. He was wearing a T-shirt that exposed the tattoos on his neck and arms, the crude monotone type that spoke of time spent inside.

Bob filmed everything. I sat next to Paige, on the periphery.

"In being a priest, Daniel is a symbol of hope to so many here," she whispered to me. "Are you religious?"

"Not especially," I replied. "I went to a Catholic school for a bit, but then we moved, and dad was cool with all that kind of stuff, never really into it. Tell me about your parents."

"Dad's a plastic surgeon. He and Mom divorced about ten years ago when I was—Jesse, how old are you?"

"Sixteen."

"Yeah, me too. Everyone else here's either heaps old, or a kid. Where's your mom?"

"I've got a stepmom too," I said. "She's not like Audrey though, mine's a dragon—and not a cool Harry Potter dragon."

"I don't think Harry Potter's cool."

"Me neither," I whispered back. "Third book was okay, though."

She smiled. "Did your mom live close by?"

"Don't know," I replied. "I've been wondering about finding her—lately. Since all this happened. I've had plenty of time to think, you know? What about yours?"

"San Fran," she said. "I visit her every two weeks. It's a short trip now—she used to live in Phoenix, which was harder. Moves around a lot."

I caught her look of doubt, as if she were questioning her own use of the present tense, so I shifted the conversation. "Do you like L.A.?"

"Where we are, yeah, I like it," she said. "Good friends, awesome weather, and we've got, like, the best beaches."

Her eyes . . . it was hard to look her in the eyes, harder still to choose which color iris to focus on.

"Mom's seeing a guy, he's okay," Paige said, a little distant in thought. "Audrey didn't used to be so cool. Actually, I kind of hated her, until all this happened. She's changed. *I've* changed. Hell, everything's changed, right?"

I nodded. The rest of the room was listening to Tom read from the Bible, his voice low and resonant, his flock nodding and believing.

"We go to church sometimes," I said to Paige, and I felt her look at me as I watched the flickering of the candles on our table. "Dad and me. No special occasion, we just might be driving by one or whatever. We go in, light candles for those who aren't with us anymore."

For a moment I could clearly see a mental slide show of all the faces of the departed. There were not enough candles in the world right now.

"That's nice," she said. Her hand under the table squeezed my leg. "We should do that, tonight—light some candles for the friends you lost."

I nodded. Was now the right time, while we were talking close like this, to ask her to leave? *I want you to leave here with me.* I went to take her hand in mine but she moved it. I looked away, at Daniel.

"You know, we're lucky here," she said. "We've got good shelter, and just about everything we need—things that might be scarce out there on the road. That's what you're dying to ask me, isn't it? Will I leave?"

"Well—"

"We have a couple of badly wounded people who can't walk—what's supposed to happen to them?"

"You could use the truck—"

"What if we can't drive it in this weather? On those choked roads?"

We watched the black clouds rolling in for the night's snow dump, the strong frozen wind fast behind it.

"I hear what you're saying . . ." I admitted.

"But you're not convinced that we're doing the right thing, are you?" Paige asked, looking at me.

I was taken aback by her question. "If it were me in your situation? Yeah, I probably would leave," I replied. What a choice. Wait until trouble comes knocking on your door here or go out and meet it head on. Who's to say which is the greater risk?

"But way out there, Jesse? On the road, like sleeping in abandoned houses or whatnot until, what, we somehow find safety?" Paige threw a golf ball out onto the snow-covered fake plastic turf. When it landed it disappeared, swallowed up by white. "I mean, for you, maybe, but for the women and the younger kids here—it's not for us."

"Yeah, it's cool," I said. "I get it."

"Totally makes sense to play it safe, yeah? At least while it's so cold and the days are so short."

She asked, "There's nothing that gives you any doubt about leaving here?"

"My two friends at the zoo? I can't leave them behind, and I can't let them wait around. I want to get them to safety."

"Didn't you say that you had another friend too—a guy?"

I thought of Caleb, and how I felt must have showed because she put her hand on mine: hers was soft and warm.

"Why don't you tell me more about Anna," she said. "I'd like to hear about her."

8

There was a sleeping hall with cot beds set up in what once had been a conference room. It was warm in here, the warmth of a dozen bodies already at rest. The sound of the snowstorm outside was a constant whirring and whistling. It almost made me nostalgic for the sanctuary of the skyscraper I'd stayed in at 30 Rock—then I remembered the creaky old building that Felicity and Rachel were stuck in right now.

"It's mainly the kids and women in here," Paige said. She went to a corner, lit by a little battery-powered lantern. "The rest are at the other side of the dining hall."

Paige sat down among five kids, two of whom I'd seen arrive that afternoon with their parents. They'd lasted two weeks in their apartment a few blocks from here and ventured out for food and fuel and, like me, decided to try this place out. Their mom was already asleep in a bed nearby, and I could hear relief in her quiet snoring. I sat next to Paige, leaning up against the wall, all the kids in their cot beds, under blankets, looking up at me with sleepily suspicious eyes. I poked my tongue out at the youngest, a five-year-old girl, and she cracked into a smile.

Paige read them *Stuart Little*. They were already about thirty pages in. She read the part where Stuart's doing his sailboat race, and then about Margalo. I really liked that story, how he protected her and his family adopted her; she flees for her life, he goes out to look for her. We don't know how it ends for the two of them, if they will ever come together again, but I'm confident that Stuart found her. I preferred stories that didn't provide all the answers.

The kids soon fell asleep, except for a boy of about eight, who was happy to lie there and watch patterns on the ceiling from the LED strip lights outside in the hall. This warm environment made for a comforting time and place. I felt as tired as I could remember. I drifted off and woke with a start, as if I had tripped.

"Looks like you need to get some sleep," Paige said. "I've set your bed up, I'll show you."

She took me through a screen of hanging sheets that acted as curtains to a row of beds. A couple of other teenagers were asleep, along with the middle-aged pair I'd seen arguing earlier.

"My parents sleep in the far corner over there," she said. "They'll be a few hours still, they're always staying up with the others. Yours is over there." She pointed, and I nodded.

"Thanks. I'll go to bed in a sec," I told her, and

watched as she climbed under the quilt, turning away from me.

I went to the bathroom, washed with some cold water and soap, brushed my teeth, changed T-shirts and put my gear in my pack, which I took with me and plunked at the end of my bed. I hung my coat on the clothes peg further down the hall. I lingered. Hesitation ran through my every fiber. I could slip out now, leave them all, head back to the zoo and figure my own way out of the city. But then I'd be forever wondering what happened to them. I wanted to wait and watch it play out. I'd give it until tomorrow. I wanted Paige to stick with her parents but it was not my place to tell her so—or to persuade her to the point where she would leave them. Was it?

I carried on further down the hall. I wanted to pick up a bottle of water, but I was also intrigued to see how the adults spent the dying hours of the day, once the children and the injured were safely tucked up in bed. The dining room was still abuzz with talk. Many bottles of wine and cans of beer had been and were being consumed. It was pretty clear that the arguments weren't any closer to being resolved.

Daniel and Tom stood up at the front. I was watching in the wings, the bottle of water steady in my hand. The difference between them was stark. Science versus God.

"All religion, my friend, is simply evolved out of fraud, fear, greed, imagination, and poetry," Tom said, pleased with himself.

"We are all free to choose our ways," Daniel countered.

"You can lead your friends into the unknown, I choose to stay here."

Paige's father looked around the room at the people who had come to rely on them both, but who might have secretly chosen one allegiance over the other.

"Nothing will get better if we stay here," Daniel said. "Don't you get that? It's dangerous." I got the sense that those who wanted to go with Daniel wanted just to be *around* him—they'd follow him anywhere.

"Perhaps. But we are comfortable here, we are sheltered—"

"Change will not come if we wait for some other person or some other time, not for the better," Daniel said. He considered the people around him, sitting and standing, listening and quietly talking among themselves. "We've been stuck here long enough."

"My outlook is more optimistic."

Daniel shook his head.

We were all getting uncomfortable at what was not being said and could see that Tom was seething about it: why couldn't those who wanted to leave, go, and those who wanted to stay, stay?

If Bob were here, he'd be taping the meeting from the far corner. I wondered what he would do with all that footage, all those little memory cards he'd pilfered from a Radio Shack. Would he edit them together one day to tell a streamlined, structured narrative? Or was this it—a raw stream-of-consciousness thing, real, hyper-real even, shaped by us all? What was it like to see life through his lens?

"*We* are the ones we've been waiting for, these people here, they have the power in them to act," Daniel said. "*We* are the change that we seek—it's in us. You should know that."

"I agree with you, Thomas, I really do," Daniel continued. "I would have liked consensus but I see that's unlikely. You do what you have to do. I'm not stopping you from staying."

"You're stopping them!"

"We're all free to choose," Daniel reasoned. "All major religious traditions carry basically the same message—"

"Spare us!"

"That is love, compassion and forgiveness; the important thing is that they should be part of our daily lives. You know these people arrived here, they found us, and more arrive every day—"

"You're stopping *her*!"

His voice was loud as a gunshot and suddenly, I turned to look at the object of the harsh accusation.

Tom's wife—Paige's stepmother, Audrey—wanted to be wherever the preacher was. She seemed sad. She knew they were fighting but could not hear it. She watched these two men and she knew they'd spoken about her because so many in the room were looking at her, Tom and Daniel included. It must hurt

Tom that she would rather be with Daniel than stay with him.

The preacher's words and oratory skills were impressive, but there was much more to him than that, and Audrey probably saw it better than anyone. Felt it. Maybe there was so much more, more than I could ever sense or see. I wondered what Caleb would have made of this power struggle. Maybe Rachel would be better equipped to handle it—this was animalistic, two bulls locking horns for supremacy.

"To hell with you, priest! To hell with your whole goddamn business!"

"Tom, I'm sorry you feel that way—"

"Don't you dare pity me!"

"Please, Tom, you will wake the children—"

"Don't sermonize me, you sonofabitch!"

"Tom, you're being—"

Screaming—a woman was screaming. The kind of scream you hoped you never heard, primal, life or death.

Bang! Daniel hit the floor. The room was silent but for the sound of two men grunting and shuffling, the sound of a man being beaten, the hush of stunned onlookers as they computed what was going down and whether or not they should do anything about it.

As I pushed through the gathered onlookers the silence broke. There were close on thirty people, several of them yelling and screaming.

Tom was on top of Daniel, punching him in the face with his full force. Daniel was on his back on the floor. His head was bouncing off the tiles, and it sounded hollow and dangerous, like a coconut cracking. His face was a bloody pulp, becoming more and more swollen with every hit.

"Get up! Go!" I said to Daniel, who rolled to his side. He stood up. Groggy. Swayed on his feet. His face was a bag of blood.

"You—"

Whatever Daniel was going to say was stopped by more violence.

I grabbed Tom as he lunged at Daniel again. But the surgeon quickly broke my hold and was punching the preacher back down onto the ground, putting all his weight into turning Daniel's face and head into a mess on the floor: a plastic surgeon undoing a lifetime's work and destroying his tools at the same time. Past, present, and future, all intertwined through an act of violence.

Maybe he was blaming this man of God for his wife's injuries, for the city or country or world being like this . . .

"What kind of god would let that happen?" Tom said. "Your god!"

I knew that if I did nothing then Daniel would die. I had to intervene.

I pulled Tom off Daniel by his shoulders. I put my hands under his armpits and hauled him back onto the hard ground. He was squirming but I had all my weight pulling down at him. He was angry, but had eyes for only one man, and he was getting up, reaching out to attack again . . .

There was a scream to my right. A piercing shriek. Audrey.

"Nooooo!"

Paige stood by the door to the hallway, neither entirely in nor out of the room, watching us. She had my pistol in her hand. It was loaded. I pulled at Tom. He fell back, wide-eyed.

Paige brought my pistol up, fired a shot into the ceiling.

Everyone froze. The sound of that gunshot resonated in me, thunder in my heart.

Tom looked around, dazed, out of it. He'd spun off the planet.

Daniel's face looked as if he'd put a gun in his mouth and pulled the trigger. There was a mess of blood on the floor.

The next sound was a kid crying in the bedroom. Then other people joined in. Some were screaming, some vomiting, many had fled the room.

I let go of Tom and walked to Paige. "It's over," I said. "Go and help Daniel."

She put an arm out and held onto mine. I stopped, looked down at her, and I had the flash recall of seeing the lifeless eyes of Anna, glass marbles on an abattoir floor. But they were unalike, really. I reminded myself of Paige's Californian tan and light, sunbleached hair, whereas Anna's hair was shiny and dark, a legacy of her Indian parentage. I blinked myself back into the now as Paige passed me the gun she was holding in her other hand.

Four men from the crowd came and hauled Daniel to the medical room. His body, being carried like that, looked like a big broken doll. Others pulled Tom away. All the fight had left him a second after that gunshot.

My hands were bloody—blood dripped and flowed off my knuckles where I'd scraped hard against the rough tiled floor in the struggle. My knees were grazed. I felt no pain. I could only think of how the sound of other people's crying had worn me out.

9

I woke up and it was still dark outside. On the bed next to me Paige was asleep on her back, her quilt down around her waist. Her California-tanned arm contrasted with the white sheets. She looked like an angel, an angel in vivid colors. I covered her, relieved that the need to talk about last night was postponed. There had to be more to say, didn't there? There had to be so much to work through . . .

I dressed quietly, and headed out. In the dining room, a few of the people were up, eating cereal. The gas burners and bottles seemed to be rationed to a hot lunch and dinner every day, and they heated water for bathing only at night. A gas heater took the edge off the room's chill but my breath still fogged in front of me. The few people awake seemed quiet and solemn, the events of last night fresh. Perhaps they'd not slept. None looked me in the eye as I took a bottle of water and a banana. The fruit was turning brown but would still be good.

There was the faintest glow of sunrise on the outside terrace and a rolling mist close to the ground at street level, but it seemed as if the Hudson's flow was the more powerful force. The pier was nearly completely covered by a blanket of fresh snow, a long slab of brilliant white jutting out into the Hudson, a lonely island of green plastic turf up against the building.

Daniel was sitting in a chair, rugged up against the cold, his eyes dark and swollen in a bandaged face, as if he were an Egyptian mummy. Bob was beside him. Two guys sitting as if they were watching the river flow by and not much to care about, if you didn't know better.

As I neared I could tell they were talking about something serious. Bob's face was tight, like he was holding back. Anger, no doubt.

"Sorry," I said, as both faced me. I shouldn't be here. "Just getting some air."

"It's cool," Bob said.

"I'll come back."

"Sit with us." Daniel motioned to a plastic chair near theirs. His voice was slightly slurred, because of his swollen lips.

"Thanks," I said, dragging the chair around to face the river. In that moment I didn't know whether to call him Father, or Daniel, or what. "I think the worst of the storm's passed."

"Maybe," Bob replied. He poured me a steaming coffee from a thermos. It had milk and a little sugar. "You rest well?"

"Yeah, very well," I said.

Daniel's eyes remained friendly. Bob's features were scary-looking in this cold dim light, like someone who'd seen it all and then some. I got the sense that this was maybe a second chance for him, some kind of fate bringing him and Daniel together. Maybe there was a guard above . . .

"I think I'll head back to the zoo today," I said, looking out at the river. The men were silent.

"You're welcome to stay with us as long as you want," Daniel said, his smiling face turning from me back to the river. "Not that it's my right to offer—I just want you to know that you'd be welcomed into the group. It's your choice."

"Thanks," I replied. I watched my cup of coffee steam and swirl. "Are you okay, Daniel?"

"I'm fine," he replied. "Don't worry about me."

We sat in silence.

"What is it?" Bob asked me. Looking more closely, I could see he looked pained, maybe close to tears, like he felt it all so raw. There was something about his eyes, not their color or their size or shape, just something about them that made me feel like they were reading deep into me. Had *he* killed someone? Did he recognize himself in me? Did he see me more honestly than I saw myself?

"Talk to us," Daniel said. "We'll listen."

I nodded. But I didn't know how to say it, how to admit it, a confession. "Just, I've—last night, it reminded me of things I've done—"

Bob said: "We've all done things."

"That's not what I mean."

"We know what you mean," Bob said. And the way he said it, he knew exactly.

I couldn't articulate it yet. Instead, I cried. Big, heaving, silent sobs. Bob took the cup from me. I leaned against him and he put a hand on my head and left it there, so gentle, so caring. I cried for a few minutes. Then I breathed deep, found composure. Tears and snot ran onto the ground between my feet. Daniel passed me some tissues.

"Thanks," I said. We sat in silence, for five, maybe ten minutes. Just the three of us out here in the elements.

It felt as if hours had passed—in a good way. As if last night's events hadn't happened. They each topped up their coffees, waited, patient. They gave me the space to sort out what I needed to share.

"I killed one of them," I said. It was an admission, a confession, as much to myself as to them. "One of the Chasers. He was coming at me. He was right at me. I had to—I didn't think I had any other . . ."

I looked at the floor through my interlinked trembling fingers, those hands that had killed. Bob nodded.

"I don't think I had a choice," I said. "But there's always a choice, isn't there? It was him or me. I chose, and I killed him dead, like that."

"God is ready and waiting to forgive anyone who asks—"

"I don't want forgiveness," I said, looking Daniel in the eye, then felt guilty at my tone. There was no judgment there, no pity nor compassion. Simple understanding. I had to live with this, to feel it, forever, that was my burden alone. Some things no amount of belief should shroud. "I just want you to know . . . that I'm sorry. That I think about it every day. I see his face, I hear the shots. I lie awake at night and it's the final thing I see. This follows me because it was me, it is me."

"Your future actions may cleanse you of this guilt," Daniel said, his voice so soft and quiet that he could have said anything and it would have given some comfort for us to reside in. "You can be pure again, for you have admitted a shameful deed so that it need no longer haunt you day and night."

"Thanks."

"If we confess our sins to Him," Bob added, perhaps repeating words he'd heard from Daniel, and whether he was speaking of himself or for me I would never know and it didn't matter, "He can be depended on to forgive us and to cleanse us from every wrong."

I nodded, but I felt like a phony coming to their God now, my hands outstretched, waiting for an offering, asking for so much in return for—what? What have I ever given? Besides, to join their flock now was to admit defeat, right? Was it that more than simply *being* alone, I *wanted* to be alone?

"I'm going to leave today," I said. "I have to get

back to my friends, make plans to get out of the city somehow."

Bob nodded. He looked at the sky. "Weather's moving in," he said. "You won't make it far out there today."

I stood and looked around: he was right—the wind was blowing a gale and the morning sky was becoming dark as night.

"Why don't you come with us?" he said. "Drop you a few blocks out."

"You guys are going out for supplies?"

Daniel gave Bob a look of approval, then the younger man said, "We're going to check something out, if you want to come."

"How long will it take?"

"Not long," Bob replied. "And I promise you this—it ain't no waste of time."

10

"Jesse, keep a sharp eye out," Bob said as he drove.

I liked riding high, in this sturdy cocoon. Bob had brought a shotgun, and I felt safe. Outside the vehicle the wind was now so strong that pieces of debris were flying through the air and occasionally smashing against the side of the truck.

After fifteen minutes we pulled up outside a small church. Bob killed the engine, but we all stayed put for a bit, watching.

"Nothing but an empty white street," Bob said. "No one will be prowling around here in this weather."

To accentuate the point a large plastic bin blew across the street in front of us like tumbleweed.

I asked Daniel, "Was this your church?"

"No," he said, looking at me in the rearview mirror. "My friend was the priest here."

"Do you know where he is?" I asked.

"No longer with us," Daniel said, his voice matter-of-fact.

We got out of the vehicle; walking was near-impossible as we leaned into the wind and pushed ahead, Bob leading the way. Inside the church the darkness retreated in the beams of our powerful flashlights.

"I take it we're not on another food trip?" I said as we made our way towards the altar.

"Something even more important," Daniel said.

"Especially to you," Bob added with a chuckle.

I followed them closely. Daniel knew where he was going and a minute later, we'd gone down two flights of stone stairs to a damp basement with the sound of . . .

Running water?

There was a stream running right through the stone floor. It was old, clearly pre-dating the building, as the floor was two feet or so above the water level and ended with rough-hewn stone walls.

"There are stories of priests here . . ." Daniel looked wistful as he spoke. "They'd come down and fish in this stream."

"No way!" I said.

"I'd believe it," Bob said, "and there are heaps of watercourses like this throughout the city, some of them real big. They feed out of the rivers, through what was once wetlands, and back into the river system. There'd be fish swimming through here, for sure."

"The water here's usually much lower than this,"

Daniel said, crouching down and shining his light into the water, and we could see the dark stain a good three feet below the present waterline. "See?"

"Yeah, I can see that," Bob said, down on his hands and knees and peering into the openings at each side of the wall where the little underground stream flashed through—quite quickly. "Yep—I'd say I was right."

"Right?" I asked, wondering about the importance of what seemed so evident and relevant to them. "About what?"

Bob, his video camera hanging loose on a lanyard around his neck, suddenly began speaking from his own authority: "Manhattan's storm-water drainage system and the sewer system were linked many years ago, so when there are torrential rains and the pipes back up—and I'm talking millions of gallons of rainwater mixed with raw sewage—the flow is routed away from the city's fourteen sewage plants and towards a web of underground pipes that empty directly into the East River, the Hudson, and New York Harbor."

"I don't get the significance?"

"Multiply the flow by ten," Bob said, smiling, looking again at the fast-flowing torrent. "Jesse, this water line here shows more than just an increased flow— and judgin' by the smell, this ain't coming from the sewer system."

"What then?"

"It's a water-supply tunnel."

I shrugged, not sure what to make of this revelation, something that seemed to be cheering him so.

"I saw that one of the older city water tunnels had collapsed, the day of the attack," he explained. "In the Lower East Side. Hell, in one section a couple of blocks had collapsed down into it."

"So what does that mean for us?" I asked. "That there's heaps of water flushing under the city, so—what, we can steer the Chasers underground, clear out the city?"

I recalled a vision of masses of them congregated in a damp subway station. Dark spaces underground were not where I'd want to be with Chasers around.

Bob shook his head. "Billions of gallons flush through every day, gravity-fed," he said, squatting down on the dusty stone floor. He shone his flashlight as he traced a finger diagram. "This here is Manhattan. There are three major water tunnels that feed the whole city—One, Two and Three. *Massive* tunnels."

I looked at the snaking lines he'd drawn.

"This is Tunnel One, which I'd seen breached." He pointed to another. "Number Two. May or may not be undamaged, but that's by the bye because there's too much risk. But *this* one—" He tapped a third line. "Water Tunnel Three. It's not fully operational yet. There's hardened access points at the relief valves here, here, and—*here*."

I could see where his finger was pointing, right in the center of the city. "In Central Park?"

"Shaft 13B," he said, tapping the diagram. "Yep, Central Park, right near the reservoir."

"And what?" I asked again. "What does this mean for us?"

"It means we get there, and we've got a safe way out."

"What?" He wanted us to go to the park and out through a tunnel—a *water tunnel*?

"It's a way out, Jesse," Daniel said. "It's a safe way out of the city."

"And—and what, we go down into the tunnel and float out with the water, like corks bobbing along?" I asked.

Bob almost laughed and shook his head.

"No. Number Three's not operational in a lot of sections as it's still being built—besides, it's traversable, by foot, along girders, even when it's flooded." He smiled, victorious. "It's like our own highway outta here!"

The possibility sent heat up my spine.

"But—but getting there," I said, "and then making our way through all those Chasers around the massive reservoir—"

Bob and Daniel nodded as if they'd well considered that point. "It won't be easy," Daniel said. "But no way out is easy."

"And, what if, what if it's collapsed, like the tunnel you've seen?"

Bob shook his head. "Maybe, but I seriously doubt it," he said. "Those other tunnels are near on a hundred years old apiece. Number Three has been under construction for half a century and it's a hell of a lot stronger than the others were when they were new. It'll be sound."

"How big are these tunnels?" I asked.

"Twenty-four feet across."

Big enough for a couple of buses and then some. Safely tucked under the city but . . .

"And how far down?"

He shuffled his feet on the floor, as if hesitating to answer. "About seven hundred feet."

"Look, Bob, the concept of getting outta Manhattan this way is great, but if you're talking about taking the whole group through here, well, you've got maybe ten people out of about forty who'd struggle to trek seven blocks in a day, let alone as far as Central Park and then *down* seven hundred feet."

"That's about the same distance as a few blocks—"

"That's not what I mean," I said, and he nodded that he knew. "Getting to Central Park is a decent trek in itself, and that's just to the *edge* of the park. You're talking about going right *into* it." I looked to Daniel. "You know I want to leave, but since I learned what happened to those guys who left—do you really think you can convince the others to join you?"

"It will be hard, Jesse," Daniel said. "But from all reports, even what you've told us, we know that there's no way out of the city that's going to be easy. The group will come around."

"This is our safest bet," Bob added. "We'll be underground, a *long* way underground, in a tunnel that's sturdy. Means we can get a long way away from the city, in a safe environment. We get to the tunnel, I can lock us in and we can rest before trekking out."

"Are you sure it's safe once you're inside?"

"Only a handful of city workers know where the entrances are—hell, I may be the only living person who remembers the combination of the access hatches."

I looked at him, our faces up-lit as the flashlights bounced their glow from the floor.

"And there's no other access points?" I asked. "Nothing closer?"

"There're shafts, yeah, at 10th and 30th—but I checked each of them three days ago, they're impassable. They're in basements of buildings and subway stations that are now piles of rubble. The relief valve hatches, like the one in Central Park, are designed to be bombproof, and it's locked up as good as a bank vault to keep terrorists from getting at the city water supply. It'll be good."

"Chasers will be all around there," I said, absently looking at the little diagram. "There's no place else?"

"Maybe we'd find another way," Bob said, "if we had time to spend searching. I mean, we could try other tunnels—there's some recent Con Edison transmission lines heading under the Harlem River, a substation up in Inwood, but I don't know exact details. I mean, we could try looking up city records—"

"The less we have to move our group through this city, the better," Daniel said, with finality. "And the sooner we leave, the better."

"That's what I think," Bob said. "I'll go scout up there at this point in the park, and if there's access and it's held, I'll come back and we set out with the group."

They looked at each other and Bob nodded, as if the two of them had had this discussion already, worked through the pros and cons, and made their decision.

"Where's it go?" I asked them. "Where's this tunnel lead?"

"We got options," Bob said. "The Van Cortlandt valve chamber complex in the Bronx—"

"That's north?"

"Yeah," he replied. "Could even follow it all the way up to Hillview Reservoir in Yonkers. Or we could even go across to Brooklyn, but I don't like that idea."

"We should decide before we get going," Daniel said.

"I'll need to go look," Bob said, standing.

"Wait—you're going *now*?" I asked.

"No time like the present."

"This weather's insane!"

"Sure—no one else will be out in the streets."

"And you'll go all the way to the Central Park Reservoir?"

"Yep."

"There's thousands of infected there."

"I'll be careful," he said, clapped my back and ran up the stairs. I turned to Daniel.

"He'll be back by morning," Daniel said. "He'll make it up there, scout it out and spend the night, then come back."

"And then you leave?"

"If he gives it the all clear, yes."

"The whole group?"

Daniel adjusted the bandage around his eyes. "I'd prefer it that way, or it might be just whoever wants to come with us."

I swallowed hard. I knew I'd have to play a part in convincing the others, which meant I was stuck with this group for the rest of the day. Felicity and Rachel would worry, but what choice did I have—this was as good as it got right now. Maybe in our absence Paige would have a word in her dad's ear; maybe Tom would come around to see the sense in leaving. He'd figure out that leaving en masse was the better choice here.

"If all's good with this, I'll need to leave earlier and get my friends from the zoo, meet up with you guys there."

"Sure," Daniel said and we walked upstairs. He walked over to the feet of Jesus on a cross, larger than life, and dipped his head and closed his eyes and prayed.

"I remember the mayor saying that the aging pipelines were vulnerable and that this city could be brought to its knees if one of the aqueducts collapsed," Daniel said, his low voice reverberating around the empty nave. "*A potential apocalypse.* Well, we're living more than that now, so I ask you, Lord, help us out of it."

11

"We'll have to pull over," Daniel said.

I slowed the truck and put it into park, keeping the engine running. The visibility was near gone, although it was only 10 A.M. The day's sky was black and the headlights of the truck only served to bounce back in our faces off the thick curtain of snowfall. At least it was warm in here.

"Do you think Bob's okay out in this?"

"He'll be fine," Daniel replied. "He can hardly see his feet in front of him, so who's going to see him?"

I almost laughed. Yeah, he'd be fine—I'd been out on my own enough, and he was at least twice my size.

"How'd Bob know all that?"

"He was working for the Department of Environmental Protection," Daniel said. "He told me he once spent three months deep under the city, with a dive team, living and working down there to repair the old tunnels. Imagine that. Living in a little house so far below this city, in a subterranean world as deep as the Chrysler Building is high. You believe that?"

"I believe anything these days," I said, "nothing seems too strange anymore."

"True. He said it's hot down there," Daniel said. "Unlike the freezing air up here at the surface, it's like seventy degrees down there, a humid mist of dust and fumes."

"Seventy degrees—compared to this, that'll be like going to the tropics for a holiday."

"Hey, look there," he said, pointing across the street. Through the snowfall I could just make out a hotel and a few shops. "Since we're stuck for a bit, how about we go check it out, see if there's anything useful?"

"Sure." I killed the engine, pocketed the keys, and we darted across the road. The wind cut at me, ice knives at my face and neck; inhaling the cold air made me feel frozen from the inside out.

"Tight fit," I said, just managing to squeeze through the lobby doors, which were jammed partly open. Daniel followed; he seemed to fit more easily.

"No way Bob would have fit through that," I said and Daniel laughed.

Illuminated by our flashlights, the place looked pristine, unlike so many of the ransacked shops and other buildings. Through a side door we looked around the type of hotel store that sold a bit of everything. I took a new watch, as the face of mine had cracked. Daniel pulled on an extra coat, and I found a couple of wheeled bags that we could fill with whatever we might find of use in the hotel.

"Let's find the kitchen," Daniel said. We went through the lobby and looked around in offices and bathrooms, emerging into a large banquet hall that had been burned out, leaving a vast black-on-black landscape. Our flashlight beams couldn't reach the far walls.

"This isn't creepy at all . . ." Our feet scrunched the charred carpet and ash-strewn floor, sounding as though we were walking through a thick blanket of autumn leaves.

"There's a door down there," Daniel said, and we headed towards a couple of shiny brass handles at the corner of the room. Our movement kicked up a cloud of dust that hung in the air like smoke.

The double swinging doors squeaked open to reveal a huge stainless-steel kitchen, untouched by the fire.

"Just grab a few things that are easy to carry," he said.

"Hallelujah!" The pantry was as well stocked as any I'd ever seen, and reminded me of an apartment back at 30 Rock. "There's enough canned and packaged food here for the whole group, at least for a couple of months."

"At least," Daniel said, his voice echoing from another storeroom.

Then the meaning of my words hit me. We had to think in terms of escape—of hours left at Chelsea Piers, not days and weeks. "But let's hope we won't need it."

I began loading the bags with blocks of chocolate and packets of crackers and jars of jams and preserves. I only filled each halfway, thinking we'd need to squeeze them through the small gap in the lobby doors. I dragged them out to find Daniel washing down a couple of painkillers with a bottle of mineral water.

"Feeling all right?"

He nodded, then we both froze. A noise. Movement.

Outside the kitchen. In the banquet hall.

I made my way across the tiled floor, pausing by the doors, in my attempt to be quiet almost knocking a fire extinguisher off its rack. I put my hand over the lens of my flashlight, dimming it.

I put my ear to the gap between the doors. There, the noise again. I reached into my coat pocket for my pistol. Shit. It was in my pack, in the car!

Silence. Had it been just shifting debris? I looked back at Daniel, who stood still with apprehension.

I turned my attention back to the doors. Deranged eyes stared back between them.

"Aaarghh!"

I fell backwards onto the floor as the double doors burst open—and three Chasers emerged from the dark. I kicked out, so that one of the doors swung with a thud against the first Chaser.

Daniel rushed and slammed against the doors, sending them back again. I scrambled to my feet. He was holding firm but they pushed against us with overpowering force and we both lost our balance, skidding across the tiles.

Another glimpse of the Chasers lit by our fallen flashlight beams—

Daniel was on his hands and knees, trying to keep the doors shut as the Chasers banged hard against them—

"Hang on!" I yelled. I hauled myself up and took the extinguisher from the rack, pulled the pin, and got back beside Daniel with my shoulder against a door. "On three, let the doors go, I spray them, then we run past them and out to the truck!"

"Okay!"

"One."

"Two—"

The doors flung open towards us with incredible force. Daniel was trapped between the wall and the door, while I faltered backwards and dropped the extinguisher.

The three Chasers burst back into the room, their lean bodies tense and ready to spring, as though they were powerful predators and we hopeless prey. They stood and took me in, their eyes darting about—

SMASH!

Daniel shoved the door into them, surprising them for just long enough—

I grabbed the fire extinguisher, aimed the nozzle and squeezed the handle. White foam erupted into their faces.

"Daniel, *go*! *Move!*"

We crashed past, out into the dark banquet hall. Without our flashlights it was pitch black except for the distant glow at the far end of the hall. We ran side by side through ankle-deep ash, the sound of the Chasers behind us. The fire extinguisher was heavy but I could not leave it behind.

Daniel yelled, "Look out!"

A Chaser emerged through the shaft of light ahead and stood there just inside the room, standing his ground, and I reached him before Daniel . . .

CLONG!

The extinguisher met the side of the Chaser's head and he fell hard.

"Come on!" Daniel shouted. I was a few steps behind him. I slipped and rolled through the ashy dust. I got to my feet to see him run through the entrance hall and then the lobby and out the tight opening of the front door. I passed the extinguisher through the gap in the doors, turned on my side to squeeze through—

"I'm stuck!" I said, panicking. My chest wouldn't get through as I was heaving deep breaths.

"They're coming!"

I looked behind me and two of the foam-covered Chasers appeared at the end of the lobby.

I was wedged halfway in and out of the doorway. I pushed and wriggled, slowly squeezing myself through.

"Pull me through!" I felt Daniel tug at my arm as I looked back and kicked out at the first Chaser, hitting him in the guts, then the second careened hard into me . . . and forced me out the door.

Daniel emptied the extinguisher at them, then he helped me to my feet. We raced across the road. I couldn't see the truck for the density of the snowfall so we ran blind, me following what I thought was Daniel's footfall ahead—

I slipped, fell hard, my head hitting something solid, and everything went red–blue–black.

12

I was woken by a pat on the arm. I could see only darkness, and I realized that the hood of my sweatshirt was over my head and eyes. It was peeled back, causing me to blink at the daylight and the face before me. It took a moment to focus and recognize Tom.

So Daniel had managed to drive back, while I'd sat in the passenger seat, my head flopping about, as if my neck could no longer support it.

"Come on," Tom said. "Grab his legs, get him upstairs."

I felt myself being manhandled out of the truck and taken inside the building. I'm not sure if I said anything in those first minutes.

Propped onto a camp stretcher, the room spinning, I saw the sun in all its brilliant overwhelming glory. For a moment I had to wonder if my journey was over, and I'd made it back to summer in Australia. Back home . . .

No, the light came from a little flashlight, shining brightly into my eyes, as Tom examined me.

"Concussion, and his head's open—pass me the sutures."

A needle homed in towards my forehead but I couldn't protest. I felt pressure but no pain as he threaded through eight, nine times, up close, somewhere around my left eyebrow. His gloved hands moved fast. I smelled coffee and soap.

"Done," Tom said. "Clean him up and look him over for any other injuries."

I felt my clothing coming off. My head raised only slightly on a pillow, I saw the lady who'd been working as a nurse yesterday. She pulled off my boots and socks, and used scissors on my jeans and T-shirt.

"I g-g-gotta start wearing a helmet."

"Shh, you'll be okay," she said.

My head ached now. My face felt numb or maybe frozen. I slapped at it, but it just made my hand ache. The nurse pulled my right glove off, but had to cut through the left. My swollen hand had doubled in size since yesterday: all five fingers were now bright scarlet and so inflamed I thought they might pop. It was the second time this week I'd seen that color in nature, the first being a bird back at the zoo's Tropical Zone. A scarlet ibis? I was glad Rachel couldn't see my hand now.

Daniel brought me a cup of hot chocolate. "Can he have this?"

The lady shrugged but I nodded.

It was good, so good, and I could just bear to hold it in my shaking right hand. By now, a few people had gathered around to look at me. I hoped I still had my briefs on.

"How do you feel?" Daniel asked.

"How-w-w . . ." my teeth chattered, "d-d-do I look?"

"Like hell."

"Yep-p-p," I replied, the steam of the drink sweet on my face. "What happ-p-pened?"

"You slipped, hit your head on the way down, and went out cold," he said, squatting by my cot and lacing a blanket over my bare torso. "Took me a while to find you in the blizzard, and I had to put you in the bed of the truck—those infected were right on us."

That explained my frozen coat and face. I hoped they hadn't cut off my FDNY coat; that thing was an old friend.

"Thanks," I said. He helped me drink some more of the warm, sweet drink, and my teeth-chattering started to lessen.

I looked around the sparsely populated makeshift medical ward. The nurse seemed to have finished her inspection. I knew she was talking, could see her lips moving. Michael Jackson's "Heal the World" was playing in my mind's iTunes shuffle—how did that work? Why that song—couldn't it have been something cooler?

The nurse and Daniel moved me over to a shower stall in a bathroom. There was a small mirror. My face was black, my neck too, hair, all covered with a thick layer of ash and dirt and grime. From the burnt-out hall in the hotel? Just the whites of my eyes and teeth shone through.

Daniel and the nurse wrapped me in a hot, steaming towel. Then she sat me on a plastic seat, and Daniel lifted my feet into a tub of warm water. The woman cleaned my face and hair, the gray water streaming onto the white tiled floor. With a fresh bucket and cloth, she gave my body a sponge bath. It warmed me inside and out. As soon as she stopped I started to feel cold again, and I was stood up, unwrapped, dried off, and moved to a bed. It was a proper bed, with springs and a foam mattress and clean sheets, and they piled blankets on me. They gave me an extra pillow, propped me up a little, and almost as soon as I blinked Daniel handed me a fresh hot cocoa loaded with condensed milk.

"Thanks."

"No problem," he replied, faintly, but I heard him. I felt the effects of the needles in my head, some kind of local anesthetic.

Tom returned. Paige's dad. Plastic surgeon Tom. I watched as the nurse spoke to him. He knelt down, took my left hand, and lifted it by the wrist. I felt as detached from the appendage as if it were a piece of dead meat. He held it, turned it, prodded it, looked concerned. Unbandaged, the jagged, deep cut was angry and inflamed.

He put my hand down to my side, and motioned to the nurse. She passed him one of those things that a doctor uses to look into ears—a light and magnifying glass in one little pointy contraption.

"Anyone else hear Michael Jackson?" I asked. Blank faces. Tom checked my ears and went back to prodding my hand. He applied some liquid. Gave me several injections into the meat of my palm.

"Daniel, help me out, man," I said. "'Man in the Mirror'? No?"

He shook his head.

Paige and Audrey appeared next to Daniel. I remembered how Paige had looked when she'd fired my gun. Now . . . now, she looked hot, dressed in tight track pants and hoody. She pulled back her hood—she'd dyed her hair. It was darker now, black-brown, contrasting with her red lips. *Hot damn . . .*

I lifted my knees a little to adjust the blankets, looked over to Tom and watched as he pulled a jagged splinter of steel the size of a two-inch nail from the heel of my palm.

"Ouch."

He looked at me, as if he was surprised that it had hurt, and went back to cleaning the wound.

"I'll give you a tetanus shot," he said. The nurse came over with a few pills and a cup of water, while Tom administered another injection. "Take those for the pain and inflammation, I'll give you a penicillin shot to kick-start things. All this may make you drowsy."

I took the pills. Tom prepped yet another syringe.

"Really?" I said. "Another one?"

He didn't answer, just swabbed my upper thigh and jabbed me.

"Gee, buy a guy dinner first."

It all seemed kind of comical, as if I were not really participating, let alone in pain and discomfort. No one was laughing, though. Audrey held onto Paige's shoulders. They both looked concerned. Especially Paige. It was really great.

"Paige, can you stay with Jesse?" Tom asked his daughter.

"Sure," she replied, beaming. She came and sat on the floor next to my mattress—to my right, away from my gruesome hand. I gave the thumbs-up to Daniel. He cracked a smile through his bandages.

"Hey, you guys," I said to Tom and Daniel, who were standing there. As well as feeling weirdly upbeat I felt a new kind of confidence to speak out. "You figured out your differences yet?"

Tom looked from me to Paige and then to Audrey. She gave him a look in return that revealed her influence over him. He turned to Daniel and briefly extended his hand. The hand was ignored. Instead, the preacher leaned in and embraced the surgeon, and the pair let go just as quick.

"I'm sorry," Tom said. "I didn't mean to—"

"I know."

That was as much as they were willing to concede to one another, but perhaps it was enough. Glancing at me briefly, maybe reproachfully, Tom took his medical gear and left the scene. Daniel looked at me too, those swollen eyes through the slits of bandages, his broken smile speaking of so much. He and Audrey left a moment later.

I felt sleepy. I was so warm and felt as if I didn't have a care in the world. Paige stroked my face and I forgot my hand. I closed my eyes and I think I fell asleep for a second or two. When I opened them I didn't know where I was—I loved that feeling, could have been anywhere. Paige leaned forward on her knees, brought her face to mine, looked close into my eyes. She kissed me. The sensation was so familiar.

"I remember you tasted of strawberries," I said, the heavy dark blanket of exhaustion falling upon me. The drugs were doing their thing. My mind working its magic. "I'm so sorry I left you behind . . ."

"Jesse?" She held my hand and watched me as I drifted to sleep.

"Sorry, Anna. I didn't mean to. I should have been there, with you, forever."

"Jesse—it's me," she leaned forward and was close to my face. "You haven't left me anywhere."

I smiled, my eyes closed. "And . . . I won't. I won't leave my friends, not here, not again."

13

I'd fallen asleep in the medical room. I think it was mid-kiss. Paige didn't seem to mind. She was there when I woke, four hours later, according to my new watch. Its face glowed in the dark, the hands and dial luminescent under my blankets. She was reading a book.

"Hey."

"Hello," she said, putting her book down and getting from her chair to help me sit up. "How do you feel?"

"How do I look?"

"Kinda cute."

"Oh, right," I said, feeling my face flush red. "Well, I feel like crap."

"Can I get you something?"

"First-class Qantas flight home?"

"Hmm, anything else?"

"Hot drink?"

She nodded and left the room.

The other patients seemed to be asleep. I wasn't entirely sure of the extent of their injuries but I could see one had a leg splinted. The nurse came in and helped me dress in some fresh clothes. I think Paige must have picked them out for me while I slept. They were all black: jeans, T-shirt, socks and jocks, with a zip-up leather jacket and boots. They were all new, still had the store creases in them, more spoils of the situation in which this city gave up everything material for its survivors.

Paige brought me steaming hot tea, and the nurse checked my hand and my temperature. My hand was feeling a little better but still resembled an overstuffed lump of meat, and I was told not to wear gloves until it healed. Fat chance of going against that advice— my palm was still swollen to about double its usual size. I swallowed another few pills, and was ready to get out of there. "Do you want to come and join the others?" Paige asked.

"Yeah," I said as we walked down the hallway. "Sorry I skipped out this morning—I mean, without saying good-bye."

"That's cool," she said. "I guessed you'd headed out with the guys, which was good: my dad needed that space. Where'd you go?"

"We went to go see about a way out . . . then this snowstorm."

"Bob's still out there—"

"Yeah, I know," she said, holding my good hand as we walked. "He'll be okay."

I nodded. "Hair looks good like that."

"Thanks," she replied. "I figured you prefer brunettes."

I'm not sure—did I? I shrugged.

Daniel was leading a prayer group seated in the little chapel. Audrey was there, in the front row. Her mouth moved and her eyes were closed as she prayed. I heard Daniel say, "God will be our judge." They nodded and smiled to show they got it, while I didn't understand it at all. I understood why and how they liked Daniel, taking comfort in his words and presence; I found that reassuring too, but I relied on a congregation of one. I wanted to be responsible for my own actions, however difficult they were to bear.

Another group, in the dining hall, was being addressed by Tom. I immediately sensed that the division between this group and Daniel's remained. I hoped it'd sort out, fast.

Paige took my hand, and I followed her out to a covered terrace where the wind blew snow in all directions.

"It's like snowmageddon out there," I said. I wondered if Bob was sheltering someplace or still pushing on.

The other teens were out here too, huddled on plastic chairs, looking out at the snow-covered driving range as if it were a movie screen, blankets around their shoulders and junk food in their laps. These guys were not like my friends Anna, Mini, or Dave, nor the girls at the zoo. This group was a little bit whack—right now, a couple of them were saying this was the End of Days or some such.

"The infected are evil—it's God's work."

The guy who said that was about fourteen. Maybe they'd had it too easy here, being remote from what was going on outside these walls. What would I be like if I'd stayed any longer at 30 Rock? Then again, maybe it was because they were simply younger than me. At fourteen I felt I knew everything, and I only knew half of that now. *Wow—what'll be left when I'm twenty? Thirty?*

"They're not evil," Paige said to him. "They're unfortunate. Until their sickness, they were our friends, our family, our neighbors—"

"Yeah, well, we've seen them kill!"

"And we've seen some of our own here kill, and I wouldn't label them as evil either," Daniel joined in. I wondered if he was thinking of me as he said that.

He'd taken off his bandages, and he looked better than I'd imagined, despite the black eyes and the cut lip, a dark bruise on his cheek, and wadding stuffed in his angry-looking broken nose. Yeah, he looked a wreck, but I'd seen far worse injuries these last couple of weeks. The bandages reminded me of what could have been.

"No one will ever fully fathom the strangeness of Man, nor the compassion, nor the love and hate that we succumb to," he said. He took a chair and dragged it over to join the group. "Give it time, my friends, live as you are meant to, act as if the less fortunate you see are your brothers and sisters, for that is surely what they are, what we all are, in this challenging time."

Paige and I wandered the complex. We came to another room where several people were quizzing a science teacher. He was animated, using a white-board, while the young kids all had paper and pens and were seated on the floor over in a corner as if their lesson was over. There was a buzzy atmosphere between the few adults and kids there to listen and ask, and this man who was prepared to give some answers or at least steer conversation.

"He just got here yesterday," Paige whispered into my ear.

I leaned against the doorway, listened to him.

"So they're not zombies?" someone asked.

"I really don't think so," he replied. "I mean, for a start, zombies don't have beards."

He let it hang for a sec and then cracked into laughter and his audience joined in. I liked this teacher.

"Zombies don't exist, or at least they're extinct or something," he said, and everyone laughed again. "Okay, but seriously: what is this? I don't know. I have ideas, opinions, but I have no way of proving anything. So let's talk about what we know for sure."

"It's a strain of the Shanti virus."

The teacher laughed. "Too much TV for you. Next?"

"It was an attack," an adult said. "Biological and conventional."

"Yes," he replied. "It was an attack—"

"By who?"

"We don't know."

"I bet it was those—"

"Opinions—we all have them, so let's stick to what we know," the teacher said. "It was an attack and it was partly a biological infection of some kind, right? It was airborne and contained to the initial ten, maybe fifteen minutes of a large-scale simultaneous attack on the city. What else do we know about it?"

"It killed the very young and the very weak," someone said.

He looked at the floor, nodded, as if he'd seen some such event firsthand.

"It can't be transferred from person to person, and it can't—"

"How do we know?" the teacher asked. Every face in the room seemed open, awaiting answers, scared. "How do we know it cannot be transferred?"

No one spoke. Even I wasn't so sure about that. I'd seen no evidence either way . . .

"Look, what I do know is that the future is up to us," the teacher said. "We here, and others like us, have to think about the generations to come after us, and say we want to make it a better place for our children and our children's children—we have to make it a better place."

"He's right," I said, and they all looked at me. "The choice is ours—we get to make this better, if we choose to. But not here, because it will get worse—

we've seen that. Here's what I know for sure: can you catch this virus still? Yes. Are the worst of the infected still out there, ready to kill for what runs in your veins? Yes. Do the other Chasers, the infected, present a danger? No. I've met them, up close. They are doomed here, and that sucks, but we can't do anything about that. I'm not gonna lie to you; when Bob comes back with good news, I'll be the first in line to leave here, because I want to see my dad again. I want to go home."

14

"I like what you said to them," Paige told me as we found a quiet space in an office. We sat on the carpet, leaning against the wall. It was an hour or so before dinner and we were eating a packet of peanut M&Ms.

"I meant every word," I said.

Paige nodded. "If Bob comes back with good news, they'll leave straightaway."

"But we still need your dad to come around."

"Daniel and all his friends and followers are working on my dad and a few of the skeptics." She paused, as if unsure whether or not that would work. "My dad was going to put it to a vote, to leave or stay."

"When?"

"Like, ASAP, probably tonight at dinner."

She studied a red M&M in her fingers. Her arm was touching mine.

"And he wants what, a majority vote?"

"I don't know. He wants a consensus, I guess."

"Maybe he wants to cover his butt in case you all

go and something bad happens—sorry, I didn't mean to sound mean."

"He just wants everyone to stick together."

"And that's great, I think that's best—to stick together."

"What you mean is, we should stick together and leave together."

"Well . . . there's something I haven't told you—"

I couldn't meet her gaze at that moment, and so she looked concerned. "Jesse, what is it?"

I told her about the soldiers. "One of them said that they'd found a way out to the north."

Again she nodded. This wasn't news, after all— Caleb had come here and shared that. She studied my face closely.

"Caleb was a good friend of mine."

She shook her head. *"Was?"*

I let out a deep breath, blinked away the residual delirium from my medical treatment.

"The soldiers had an unexploded missile in the back of their truck—left over from the attack." I looked at the tub of multicolored M&Ms between us. "Caleb and I were close by, and there was an attack and the missile went off."

"It . . . killed them all?"

I shook my head. After a moment she got it.

"The virus?"

"Caleb was closest. I ran. I had to. He—"

"He's one of *them*."

I nodded.

"He's—he's one of the *chasing* kind, isn't he?"

"Yeah."

She looked like she was going to throw up.

"And it might happen again, at any moment—there could be an unexploded missile or some of the contagion close by—"

"Stop it."

"I'm just saying—"

She spoke to the floor: "You know those guys who tried to leave were attacked."

Damn. I'd hoped she wouldn't have been told that, but I guess news traveled fast around here.

"My dad tried to stop them from leaving."

"They knew what they were doing."

She hesitated.

"My dad was out on the food party that day," she said.

I didn't know what to say. Or what to think. What did she mean—did she suspect her dad of killing them? Why would he do that, to prove a point? To force the rest to stay? I let her reside in a moment of silence, willing her to continue, but she didn't.

"If you knew anything about that, would you tell me?"

She nodded. She didn't look at me, but she nodded. "You don't need to convince me to leave," she said, her arms wrapped around her legs, her knees tucked under her chin. "But what if Bob comes back and tells us something that makes people think it's safer to stay here? It'll be even harder then."

"Your dad would feel justified."

"Please, Jesse, can't you speak to him?"

"That's not my place."

"Please, he might listen to you."

"Why do you think he'd listen to me?"

"Because *you* intervened in the fight. Because *you've* been outside—seen people, talked to them."

She looked at me and she held my gaze.

"Tell my dad about the group of soldiers you met," she said. "Tell my dad about them before it gets worse around here. Last night, Jesse, what my dad did to Daniel? We're turning on each other. First this attack, the infected, the weather, the other survivors—now we're turning on ourselves . . . Please."

"Okay," I said. "Okay."

Dinner was rowdy. Expectant. Feverish. Voices were raised and arguments were spreading like little wildfires, flaring here and there, then gone again, only to flare up once more and travel around the packed tables like a wave. This room had been something of an oasis last time I'd eaten here. Calm, communal, nurturing. How things had changed.

Many people wanted to leave—up to twenty-five now. Daniel sensed a consensus was so close that he had organized a few people to start packing supplies on some improvised wheeled carts. Whatever news Bob brought, *they'd* be leaving; either tomorrow or soon. They'd seen and heard enough.

The old juice lady passed and I heard her say:

"Somewhere *warmer*. Somewhere *safer*. Somewhere *better* than here—anywhere better than *here*."

That was the crux of their argument, their sound-bites, their best-of reel: Did they really grasp that this was life and death, the highest stakes there could be, with no room for error?

"I'm sick of this city!" a guy yelled. I recognized him: he'd been tending to their small stock of fire-arms when I first arrived. "Before all this I mean. There's—everything is surface, don'tcha think? And look at it now—we're living in a world where we're entitled to go out there and get some. Let's go shoot some people who are worse off than we are. Who gives a damn? They're a lesser class of human beings, the new minority. If they get in my way . . ."

I didn't have the heart to tell him that they weren't the minority, we were. I hoped his disposition and opinion wasn't contagious. You needed to be alert out there, open to surprise, not driven by rage and re-venge.

"The hell with it all—and the hell with this place," he continued. Well, at least he had spirit. "Let's get outta here!"

We walked between the tables, and loaded up our plates with more of the delicious food on offer. After we'd eaten, we walked up to Tom at his table. I had a bad feeling about this.

"He won't listen to me, he doesn't like me—" I said to Paige.

"He doesn't know you well, but he'll listen, he listens to everyone," she said. He knew me well enough to know that I fancied his daughter—wasn't that reason enough not to talk to him? But Paige had already dragged me over until I was almost in arm's reach.

Tom sat on the edge of a table talking to a group that consisted of nearly every adult at the piers. He stopped talking, looked at me.

"Tom, can I say something, to everyone?"

In public, with everyone watching, he was generous and open. Maybe he was keen to save face after the fight. "You don't have to ask—"

"I met a group of guys a few days ago," I said, scanning every face as I spoke. He seemed a little miffed that I didn't wait for the full answer to my rhetorical question. "They were dressed like US soldiers. They were walking, armed with assault rifles, with a couple of heavy trucks. Two days later I saw them motoring north, with one of the unexploded missiles from this attack in the back of their truck."

They listened, all of them. Thirty-something adult faces turned towards me.

"One of them had told me that if I were to leave, not to head south or west, not to head anyplace warmer—"

"Why?" Tom asked.

"Because this virus is worse there," I said. "He said the warmer the climate, the worse the infected are."

Tom shook his head, and there was murmuring among the group.

"That all?" Tom asked.

"He said to head north, where it's colder."

"Old news," he said. "We heard that from some-place else, Jesse. This is where we need to wait it out."

He went back to arguing, to putting forward his case to stay put. Tom wanted to stay, maybe to help those who kept turning up—there were at least three unfamiliar faces here and they'd obviously integrated well, as everyone seemed to, so quickly—maybe just to stay in a place he thought he knew. Here they had beds and warmth and food and security.

"I know you heard it before," I said, but he didn't hear me as he was talking loudly at the same time, "But what if you're wrong? What if there's no 'wait-ing out,' beyond waiting to die?"

"We've heard enough, thanks. We'll make our own decisions."

"I have to tell you something," I said.

"You *have* to?"

"Your daughter asked me to."

He looked past me to Paige.

"Please listen to him, Dad."

"I don't care if you listen to me or not," I said to Tom. I stood right next to him, at the head of the table, so that I could be heard by everyone seated there. Daniel was at the far end, and his congregation looked on in particular interest.

"You all do what you have to do, decide your own destiny. But I want you to know what I know, be-cause it may help you make your decision."

Most people nodded in acknowledgment.

"I've been here since the attack, just like you," I said. "I've lived through hell, just like you. But you know what else? I met these soldiers. And one of them did tell me to head north, if I could. That things would get worse here. And you know what? Things *have* got worse here."

There was a murmuring of agreement.

"Thanks for that," Tom said, dismissing me. "Now—"

"There's one more thing—"

"That's fine, thanks, kid—"

"Give him a moment," Daniel said, and every face at the table turned to me—Tom could see that, as clearly as I could. "What else, Jesse?"

"These soldiers were transporting a missile out of Manhattan when it was hit by a US drone aircraft," I said, talking quickly. The murmuring stopped and the group watched me, waiting for more. "A US un-manned aircraft. Attacking their own men on the ground. The missile from the aircraft hit the truck and detonated the missile left over from the attack. It was a huge explosion."

I looked down to the end and was surprised to see that the look on Daniel's face was mirrored by pretty much everyone else at the table. They all wanted to hear every little detail.

"The explosion set off the virus."

Some chairs moved at that, perhaps out of fear, to get away from me.

"I know you were told that there was a path clear to the north because my friend told you," I said. "My friend, Caleb."

I could tell there was recognition there, even on Tom's face.

"Caleb was there with me that night. He was closest to the explosion."

"No!" a lady yelled.

"He became . . . he's infected. He's infected and because he was so close to the contagion, he became one of the—he's one of the deranged ones."

The woman gasped again. Others murmured to their neighbors. A couple of people began to sob.

"He's lost. He's gone." I stood by Tom and looked him square in the eyes. "Given the chance he'll hunt you down and drink what's in you. Hell, he'd kill me too, given the chance."

The room was silent.

"That's what's here. That's what I've seen. That's a big part of why *I* want to leave." I looked all around, every face attentive, an assembly of truth. "If there's a way out of here, off this island and out of this city, I'm *taking* it. Whether it's Bob's water-tunnel plan or something I have to engineer myself, I'm outta here. That's all I know. It might not be any better, it might kill me, but it's what I have to do. Whatever is ahead of me, it's the choice I make."

I could hear the people around me breathing. But I felt as if I was holding my breath. I knew the words that were coming next, because I'd said them before to Paige—I'd said them to anyone who had listened to me. Didn't seem to make them any more real. But I liked the fact that they seemed to mean something to these people who were hearing them for the first time. It gave me a kind of hope.

"You decide what you want. Follow your heart, your mind, your gut, whatever. Me, I just want to go home."

15

"**C**ome on," Paige said. "Let's sit someplace quiet."

"After you." I followed her out to an office, and she lit a candle on the table between us. We could still hear the hum of conversation outside but not the details.

"How's your head?" she asked.

"Fine, thanks."

"Hand?"

"It's still there."

She laughed.

"Thanks for helping me out with it."

"That's cool. Thanks for speaking out back there."

Paige asked if I wanted a drink of vodka and orange but I stuck to my Coke. On her second glass I could see she changed a bit; she sat differently, looked at me weirdly, started to touch my leg under the table.

"If we're going tomorrow," I said, "I'll have to leave first thing to get a head start, to go collect Rachel and Felicity.

"Yeah . . ."

She rested her chin on her hands and looked out to nothing, a middle distance somewhere in the dark hallway.

"What is it?" I asked, pushing my glass to the side.

"What you said, about me being with my dad and Audrey."

Oh, right. That.

"You still think I should stick with them, no matter what?"

"It's your decision to make."

"But that's what you think?"

I bit my lip and she looked at me and I shrugged.

"That's what I think," I admitted. "Besides, wouldn't they make you stay?"

"They can't make me," she said, finishing her drink. "I can do—"

I put my finger to her lips, and she kind of melted into it.

"Think about it more in the morning," I said. "Don't stress about it now. Wait and hear what Bob says when he comes back. Wait and see what your dad ends up deciding to do."

She said, looking at the floor, "If we split up, I want to go with you, wherever you go."

I was touched by the trust she placed in me. At the same time, my conscience told me I had to turn her offer down. I couldn't separate her from her parents. So was I now telling her to stay? The words came reluctantly.

"Look, I still think that if your parents aren't going, you should probably stay with them, otherwise—"

"Jesse, I want to be where you are."

I swallowed hard.

"Paige—"

"I'd follow you, regardless. Understand?" She looked at me closely.

"You'd regret it, being separated from them. And it's safe in here, this place. I'm not worried for you here. Those infected people can't get at you here."

"The uninfected could."

Of course they could, we both knew it. It was a dumb thing for me to say, selling the safety of this place.

But that wasn't what was bugging me the most right now. Paige's devotion was great—what wouldn't I have given for one of the girls at school to say that kind of thing to me?—but it put an extra pressure on me that I hadn't had before. Sure, I had told myself that everything I was doing wasn't just for me, but for others too—the little communities I had managed to pull together—but was that really true? In the end, I always went off *alone*. From circumstances, but from choices, too.

If I took Paige with me, my goal would become even more crucial. But what if the end result wasn't good enough for her—or for me? I could promise to take her "home" but I couldn't guarantee what home would be like. All of a sudden, it seemed a weird and unfamiliar concept.

"Besides," she said. "I'm sick of *safe*. We're all sick of *safe*."

I leaned away from her a bit so that I could use my right hand to turn her face to mine. She had tears in her eyes. "Paige, I don't want you to—look, if you leave your parents, you're *leaving home*, yeah? You'd be losing something that you may not be able to ever get back."

I was silent, hoping the words would make sense to her.

"And?" she challenged me.

"I don't want anything to happen to you," I said. "That's what I'm scared of. You go out there, with forty people even, you have to be prepared to do whatever it takes to survive."

"I can look after myself."

"Can you?" I didn't want to dissuade her, but I had to make her look at the facts. "You come across even a small group of armed guys, they might kill you or worse."

"Worse?"

"You know what I mean."

"You're being stupid."

"Paige, whatever your parents decide, stick with them," I said. "They're the two people who'll stay with you, no matter what. They will never leave you behind, you got that?"

I knew then from her eyes that she got it, but also she wasn't sold. I hadn't even convinced myself—I mean, how could I? But Paige seemed to have made up her mind and be content with it. It really was what she wanted, and maybe it was the bravest choice anyone could make in this new earth: she'd been brave enough to find a new home. The problem was where she'd found that: in me.

16

I couldn't sleep that night, and nor could most of the others. I helped them pack and it was apparent that they had enough food and gear to survive easily for a couple of weeks on the road, if it came to that.

With dawn approaching, I worried about Bob. Would he be back? I hadn't really considered before what we'd do if we had a day of . . . nothing. Of Bob failing to return.

I lay on my bed, next to Paige. We were silent but for the occasional whisper. We tried to sleep and maybe she eventually did. A couple of hours of staring at the dark ceiling and I was convinced: *This morning, Bob will make it back.* He had street smarts, was under no illusion about the dangers out there. Unlike so many survivors, he could take care of himself. I wished the same for my two friends waiting back at the Central Park Zoo, but with every second of sleepless thinking, my worry for them grew.

It didn't rate worrying about yet. *Deal with it when*

it comes. Whatever Bob's news, I'd head back to them at first light.

Before sunrise I crept out to the food hall—the urns were already steaming and I could hear a generator humming on the terrace. I took a coffee and sat outside at a table where Bob often rested, before a box of photographic equipment: wires and memory sticks, batteries and video cameras. I flicked through the contents: he'd labeled the little memory cards with dates, and some had titles. I stopped at one marked: THE ATTACK.

I popped it into a little Sony cam and hit play but it took me a few battery changes to get the camera working.

The picture showed a dark space, then the big flare of a fire. It looked like—a church? There were sounds of sirens and screaming. Then the narration started, in Bob's urgent voice:

"The attack was ten minutes ago, I was in the confession booth here at St. Pat's Cathedral in Midtown Manhattan."

The camera panned to show a hole in the roof, then zoomed to the floor. It took a moment for the lens to focus. Sirens wailed in the background.

"This here's a missile that came in through the roof!"

I felt sick in my stomach. There was a scream off camera, and I could tell he was hesitating, maybe checking into it, then resumed:

"This missile—it hasn't exploded. I'm going to check it out, look for markings—"

His hand reached out in front of the lens—towards the missile! He shifted a piece of broken timber, revealing the side of the long steel cylinder; it looked as if a panel had come free . . .

"This is—I can see inside the missile," his voice said. *"Wait."*

It was hard to make anything out, then there was a lot of movement on the screen and the picture was suddenly bright and clear—he'd switched on the camera's light.

"Okay. Here, inside the missile, what looks like strands of big glass marbles."

They certainly did look like that. Bright red marbles, connected like a string of pearls.

"I have no idea what they are. Explosives maybe?"

There was a shrill scream off-screen and then the footage went blank.

I switched off the camera. I figured what those glass balls were: *They housed the contagion.* St. Patrick's Cathedral? That was right across Fifth Avenue from 30 Rock! All that time, it had been in there. The camera shook a little in my hands. There could be heaps of such unexploded missiles in the city—maybe the attack was meant that way—like they were on timers to detonate or something, and they'd keep going off . . .

"Ahh!"

Paige startled me—she'd put a hand on my shoulder.

"You okay?" she asked.

"Yeah," I said, ejecting the memory card from the camera. "Yeah, sorry, you just spooked me."

"Come on, I've got to show you something."

She'd put on a big coat, motioned me to follow her. I took my FDNY coat, now heavy with the pistol in the pocket, from atop my bag in the hallway.

Paige and I stood on the cold rooftop. It was still dark, the faintest glow of a new dawn on the horizon. We were alone. Paige huddled close to me as she steered us to a telescope and pointed to a spot across the Hudson.

"Ha!" I said.

"What?"

"I've seen those lights come on once before," I said, thinking about that section of New Jersey I'd seen all lit up. I'm glad that wasn't in my mind, like so much else had been back at 30 Rock.

"They came on last night," she said. "Is that when you saw it?"

I shook my head. "Almost a week ago. That's why I was making for the 79th Street Boat Basin, to try and get across."

"Think it's survivors, or automated?"

"No way to tell," I answered. I did a full sweep of the area with the telescope: nothing seemed to be moving, nothing seemed to signify that there was life over there. "Not from here; have to get closer."

I felt her pushing against me, an arm around me.

"I just want you closer," she said, her head resting

on my shoulder. By the little light of the dawning sky, I could see her watchful eyes twinkling up at me. I bent down and kissed her. I felt hot and hungry and—she smelled and tasted like strawberries. Had I imagined it? She kissed me back. I pulled away, touched my lips—she did have lip gloss on. It evoked so many memories.

"Strawberry," she said. "It's what you like, isn't it?"

She leaned in again and I kissed her. I felt a tear roll down her cheek and into my hand. I'd be lying if I said I didn't think of Anna as I kissed her. That I'd wished that she was more like Anna, but an Anna in natural colors. Suddenly, all I saw was Paige's dyed hair. Her bright red mouth.

"I can't," I said. I walked to the other side of the roof, looking down onto the street.

"What if you leave today and I never see you again?" she said, coming up behind me.

"Don't say that."

"It's a possibility, though, isn't it?"

She came close and made to kiss me again.

"Paige—I can't."

"Then think of her."

"What?"

"Anna. That's what you want, isn't it? She's who you want."

"Why are you doing this?" I asked her.

She was silent.

"Anna's gone, Paige."

"I'm here."

"Are you?" I said. "Or are you so busy being something you're not, you're forgetting who you really are?"

She looked away from me. "I thought you'd like it."

"I like you, Paige, for who you are."

"Really?"

"Why wouldn't I?"

She chewed at her bottom lip. "I wanted to know how it would feel."

"How what would feel?" I asked.

"To be loved so much—the way you loved Anna."

"She's dead, Paige. I liked her, sure, but I talk about her like that because she's dead." I gave her a hug. "Believe me . . . you got the better end of the deal."

It was easier to understand Paige now; she wanted to feel something other than desperation and loneliness. She was hungry for love, to be cared for, to be wanted, to have someone to call her own. She was with this group and she felt lonely. She wanted a different future, but I couldn't offer her that.

I no longer had a sense of home. For as long as possible, I'd been thinking of my dad and friends in Melbourne, even my stepmother, waiting for me to come back. But that didn't feel like home anymore. My idea of home had shifted—from 30 Rock, to the zoo, maybe even to here . . . wherever my friends were. For all that I had arrived trying to persuade the others to leave, how ready was I? Two days could easily slide into three, into four, even longer . . .

"Jesse?"

"Yeah?"

"Look!" She pointed to the street. "Can you see that?"

Where we stood on the roof we could see the rising sun chasing away the shadows. I followed her pointed finger, searching for—

A lone figure, on the street, running towards us, fast.

"It's Bob!"

I ran downstairs. Ran through the receiving bay, to the front roller door, started to hoist it open before he even had to bang on it.

He waved, too exhausted to talk, doubled over with his hands on his knees.

I looked out the door, up and down the street: it seemed clear, quiet.

"Bob, you good?"

He stumbled through and heaved down on the chain to close the door.

"Bob?"

"Tell—the others—tell them," he gasped for air, "we're going to be attacked!"

17

"I tried to lose them," Bob said to me and the six other guys who had instantly assembled on the roof. "Shit."

The vehicles came to a screeching halt out front, two big four-wheel drives, each carrying maybe eight men. The guys poured out, dressed in mismatched snow gear. Most had automatic rifles.

"What do we do?" I asked, fingering my pistol and keeping below the parapet of the roof. I saw a couple of our guys had shotguns, another had an old-looking rifle, the rest pistols of some sort. "I don't think we can take them on in a firefight."

Bob nodded his agreement, though the other guys didn't look sold. Hell, what choice did we have?

"Maybe if we start shooting all at once, it'll scare them off," I said. I could see them attaching a cable winch from a vehicle to our roller doors.

"We can do better than that," a voice said. I heard the rattling of glass and looked across.

"This," the science teacher said. He set down a case

of bottles filled with some kind of flammable liquid with rags sticking out. "Light and throw—careful not to drop one around here."

All eight of us each took a bottle, which I could now see had smaller lidded mini-bar bottles of another liquid inside them. The teacher held out a flaming blowtorch and the fuses lit.

"Now!"

We tossed the firebombs over the lip of the roof.

CRACK CRACK!

A series of gunshots rang out our way. We heard glass shattering and people yelling as flames engulfed the street below. Light and heat filled the sky. Bob looked over the edge.

"They're bugging out!" he said.

I stole a glance. They piled into the other four-wheel drive and tore off down the road as the dark smoke rose.

"Come on, don't breathe the smoke!" the teacher said, and we followed his lead by covering our faces as we ran across the roof and headed downstairs. What little smoke already hit us burned at my eyes.

"What was in there?"

"Trade secret," the teacher replied as we reached the landing on the terrace below. "But it included chlorine."

"They're gone," Tom said, approaching us with another group of armed guys. "But I'm sure they'll be back, and better armed than before."

"We'd better put that fire out," the teacher said, moving off with a few of the guys.

Tom looked accusingly at Bob, and part of me relished this turn of events: if there was anyone who needed to be convinced of the increasing dangers of remaining at Chelsea Piers, it was Tom.

"Bob," I said, "tell us—what did you find out there?"

Daniel joined us, and Bob looked at us all and smiled.

Everyone had assembled. Nerves settled. Excitement crackled.

"It's right here," Bob said, marking a spot on the map of Manhattan spread out on a table in the food hall. "The Central Park access hatch to the relief valve."

"And?" Daniel asked.

"And it's fine!"

Cheers spread through the room like wildfire. Tom remained silent. People came over and crowded the map.

"How about the park?" I asked.

"Sorry?" Bob replied over the cacophony.

"The park—the reservoir," I said, motioning to the map that showed his pen mark of the tunnel access, a dot on the northern shoreline. "It's still full of Chasers, right?"

"Around the reservoir, yeah," he said, "thousands of them." He added, "By day I only saw the docile ones, hanging around the water supplies. Wasn't until dusk that I saw a few groups of the other kind appear. They picked off the weaker ones at the edges of the groups."

"Then we move fast, while it's light," Daniel said. "We can follow this water tunnel all the way out!"

Tom stormed away, but Audrey caught him by the door. Once again, she tried to temper his mood, to persuade him to think more rationally.

"They'll be at it all day," I said to Paige.

"Yep."

She looked at her dad sitting there with Audrey, nodding in silence as he read her notes, as if Daniel and Bob's words were finally sinking in.

"What if everyone leaves but us?" she asked.

"Paige, it'll be fine: they'll come around, you'll see." I put my bandaged hand to her face. "Your dad's just making a show of taking in all the pros and cons to save face."

She nodded. "What if those guys come back?"

I looked around at all the men here. Despite the attack just now—or maybe, in a way, because of their success in repelling it—they were smiling and going about their tasks with a new sense of optimistic urgency.

"Nothing will crack this spirit of survival," I said. "You've got plenty of weapons to ward off an attack. The danger would be if the attackers wanted to come back and create a siege and you couldn't get out." I motioned to the guys who were on weapons duty:

they had a couple of trestle tables filed with firearms and makeshift bombs. "But like I said, you've got enough to fight off anything. You'll be fine."

She smiled but I could tell from her face that she was not completely sold. That was okay. A bit of nervous doubt, of uncertainty, kept you on your toes.

I slipped my pack over my shoulders.

Daniel's last look at me spoke of a fear for his group as well as an acceptance of the worst that might happen. But he knew that there was a fate that befalls people unless they act. It had nothing to do with a belief in a god or otherwise.

Bob shook my hand. His eyes were black orbs peering out of an expression of hope and expectation. He'd seen so much already. Was there any scenario that he couldn't be prepared for? I would have loved some parting words of wisdom from him, but perhaps it was best not to ask. Dwelling on the past would be of no real use to us now.

"Three hours after dawn tomorrow," he reiterated.

"See you soon," I said, and left it at that.

Paige walked me out through the roller door, where two armed guys stood guard, watchful over the street outside. The attackers' vehicle was a smoldering wreck covered in fire foam. Several other guys, recruited from among the adults left inside the building, stood sentry on the roof. I waved back at them.

Where were they the other night, those able men at the ready to defend? Were they so gripped by the bystander effect that they stood there and let the attack on Daniel occur, content to let someone else do something about it? Had this city learned nothing after all this time, after all this? Was it too much to hope for a time where we would stand up for one another no matter the cost, just because it was right?

"You'll meet us at the park?" Paige asked.

"Yep, I'll be there," I replied. I adjusted my coat, looked up and down the empty street, the burn marks on the road still smoking. Before Bob had returned, part of me wanted to say to Paige, *Pack and get dressed, before your father hears us. Follow me.* But I knew that was just sleepless fantasy.

Through the open roller door I could see Bob was fueling up the big Ford pickup truck. They'd pack it full of gear and passengers; they had tried to make the wounded and elderly as comfortable as possible. The rest would walk after it. "Three hours after dawn tomorrow—Bob reckons it'll take you that long to get there."

"I can't bear to think about you out there on the streets alone," said Paige.

"I'll be fine," I replied, a smile full of genuine hope and what tomorrow's dawn would bring. "Done it plenty of times. You just be careful—stick close to the group, and be wary—the sound of that truck will attract attention."

"I've got over forty people with me."

"You're right, but don't for a moment fool yourself—it's dangerous out there," I said, touching her cheek. "No matter what, stay with those who can protect you—" I added, seeing Bob cleaning a shotgun. "See you real soon, okay?"

I gave her a hug and pried myself away quickly.

"Jesse—"

"I'll be there," I said, my teeth chattering. It was cold today, perhaps clearer and colder than any previous day. There was such a chill. "Just show up. All of you, in one piece. I have to go get my friends prepped and ready. I can't leave them behind."

Because I've done that once and I know how it feels.

"Can't I just come with you now?" she said, looking back into the building. "They won't mind—"

"Paige, I'll see you soon."

"Can't we—"

"Paige—"

"I don't want you to go alone."

I hugged her. She cried. She was warm and her body was shaking.

"I need you," she said.

What could I say to her?

"Look, I'm sorry we have to go separately," I said. "But it's not for long, I promise." I hoped she understood. "We have to do this, this way, to find something better."

She nodded with a small smile as she wiped her nose on her sleeve and said, "I've found something better."

"Me too," I said, and I turned and left.

Something beautiful, something rare: I'd found her.

But she wasn't mine to have. We didn't belong to each other; we didn't belong to anyone, except ourselves. Had I finally discovered the meaning of home? Was it inside me—did I carry it, wherever I went?

"Jesse!"

I turned.

"Tom?"

He ran over, Paige close behind him, in tears.

"Change of plan," he said. "If we're going, we go ASAP, before those sons of bitches come back and attack us again."

"When are you leaving?"

"Two hours."

I checked my watch. Two hours' head start . . . I was at least twice as quick as them. It'd do. I could make it.

"Then I'll see you at the park soon," I said. Paige clung to her father's arm.

"Bob says we can be there by 2 P.M.," Tom said. He shook my hand, and I turned and ran.

"See you at two!" I yelled out.

"And Jesse?"

I turned.

Tom said: "Thank you."

18

It was just 9 A.M.

I looked back before rounding the corner of West 21st. I was alone again; I'd grown so used to walking these streets by myself that I felt more at ease this way than I would with someone tagging along. I wanted to tell Paige not to worry about me but it'd be like trying to tell her not to grow up too fast—I knew that was too little, too late. I wanted to tell her to enjoy and make the most of the time she had, because you never know how long you have left, and you need to live fast—but take time to see everything around you as well. A mantra for being out here on the streets. A mantra for going it alone.

There was a ball of excitement in my gut as I jogged.

I imagined seeing the group this afternoon, amassed at the top of the reservoir; imagined heading down into the bowels of the earth, like some kind of image from *The Hobbit*. Dad had read me the illustrated version he'd had as a boy. I think I was about six or seven. He'd read me Bilbo's adventures and I'd dream so vividly each night that I was entering that world, Middle-earth, that I was part of the fray.

A noise made me turn.

Nothing.

I stopped and listened. Debris settling somewhere in a building, maybe. I was passing the theological seminary, where Daniel had worked. Unlike St. Pat's, this place hadn't been so lucky—maybe a quarter of the structure was still standing, the rest snow-covered rubble.

A life-size poster of a girl in an advertisement, maybe from a bus stop or billboard, was lodged in the snow upright, so that it resembled a person walking by me. It reminded me of Paige. But her fate remained elsewhere, determined by her parents and, if she was lucky, herself.

I kept moving. I turned north at Seventh Avenue. I tried to keep up a steady run, settling in to a rhythm through the ankle-deep snow, slow enough to dodge over and around obstacles.

To see the girls' faces, back at the zoo, when I told them that we'd be leaving—*leaving under the city!*— man, that was going to be awesome. I needed to get back to Rachel—I'd worried about her, even if she did have Felicity there now to help with the animals. How'd she been coping these last couple of days? I looked forward to telling them about all those people at Chelsea Piers.

After stopping to check that the coast was clear, I

started to run eastwards along 23rd. I had a slight limp in my right leg, my hands hurt, and the grazes rubbed raw against the material of my black jeans.

I thought about when Tom was beating Daniel. Maybe Paige got it but the rest, about thirty adults, had just stood there and watched, helpless. That's when I had decided for sure: *This group is not me and I want no part in it, no future with them. I'll leave with them as a means to getting a step closer to home.* These people were *not* my future—and Paige was caught up in that.

I paused at an intersection at Fifth, to do my listening and watching routine. All clear. My breath was massive heaving bursts of steam. I walked north. Fifth Avenue, the homestretch. I could hear my heart drum in my ears.

It was cold in these streets. There was a fire burning in a park to my right and there were so many things I wished I had said to Paige; I could have held her longer or run away with her in the night—she might have done it, she was throwing herself at me and clearly seeking salvation from those people, from something I didn't understand the gravity of until that moment of violence, and the inert bystanders.

This was a strange city, as it was, as it remained.

In Rockefeller Plaza I stood under an awning and watched the white snow fall. It was light, soft, floating in a windless day. I didn't feel the cold anymore. I leaned against the stone wall. I'd made good time here. Watched and listened to the day unfold as I caught my breath. Still no sign of Chasers, no sign of life out here other than my own.

This was where, almost three weeks ago, during a tour of Manhattan, I had taken shelter with Anna. It was a miserable morning, cold and dark and windy and full of hard rain; we'd rested here while the others ran to the underground mall or whatever, down near the ice-skating rink, and we'd huddled in close.

Her breath smelled of strawberries and she looked at me and we kissed . . .

I thought of that other group. Paige and her stepmother, the preacher. All of them. Bob and his camera. I wondered what someone would someday make of the footage of me. What about last night, the one time there was no video rolling, a blank patch in his recordings? There was one being who perhaps had seen all that, seen all this, seen the past and the present and saw me right now. Had He seen the future and still let it happen? I decided it was time to go find out. Just for a moment. Confront a fear. Lay some blame. Learn something new. I checked my watch. Yes, I had time.

19

Manhattan was dry today, just the light falling of snow and a mist that now hung several feet above street level, like a light box radiating a dull, uniform gray glow. The snow-covered fire engines were the same as before. That massive crater where the ice rink used to be remained undisturbed.

The familiarity of these streets was reassuring. There were no fresh corpses blood-spattering the clean snow. No curling trails of smoke or smoldering embers from new fires. No acrid stench of chemicals or melted plastic. If there was a second act to be played out, it hadn't happened yet. We still had time.

It wouldn't take the girls and me long to get to the rendezvous point. But that was assuming all was well at the zoo, that we could just pack and go, and that Felicity and Rachel hadn't suffered an attack like the one at the piers.

I weaved between smashed and destroyed vehicles and in and out of shattered storefronts. I stopped to listen to the quiet. If the streets remained like this,

I knew I could follow Fifth all the way to the zoo real fast. I put my shaking hands in my coat pockets. Which was more alarming—the cold or the nerves, the excitement of what was to come?

Previously when I'd walked north, I'd been always wary, always prepared, always looking for something I might need; not today. I stopped under the awning of a deli-cum-café and looked inside. But I felt no need to go in and forage for supplies. I didn't want to be burdened with the provisions that meant I had a long stay ahead of me. I felt light on my feet now. My pack and me and the streets around me, all of it seemed more manageable. It was liberating. No more tomorrows in this place.

"My last day in this city."

I spoke out loud, but I wasn't kidding myself that there were people listening. I was addressing the one person I could rely on: myself.

"This is my last day here!" The words echoed around the streets. "Here—here—here!"

A moment later, they were replaced by a rumbling that I thought was a building coming down, except that it reverberated, as if it was happening all over again—then faded. Some kind of engine? An aircraft? I kept moving, heading away from the noise. I couldn't be distracted.

Under the last bare-branched tree at Rockefeller Plaza I paused to catch my breath. Snow crunching underfoot was the only sound audible. At least I'd hear something sinister coming. I found a baseball bat in the back of someone's car and hit snowballs with it as I walked. It was almost easy to forget the dangers around me.

"Good-bye, 30 Rock."

I'd lived in that tall building for twelve days, and I was thankful for everything that it provided. I remembered the last time I was here, thinking that I could climb up those sixty-five levels and get into my warm bed. But I wouldn't do it, ever again, because I didn't want to alter my memories of that place. Even if this city was fixed and life went back to some kind of normal, I would never go up there again. Right now, there was no room for nostalgia. Why reminisce?

I took a bottled juice out of my backpack and allowed myself a moment to drink it. There was graffiti on a glass storefront, a row of people in black spray-painted stencil-work. A guy in the center was the biggest image, the rest fading into the background. He stood about my height, maybe a rifle in his hand. His face was really just a few sharp black lines of spray-paint.

I read some of the graffiti. I wondered if it would still be called that in the future. Maybe writing on walls would be the new literature of this world. We'd had no newspapers, no magazines since the attack, and maybe we wouldn't again. Maybe, somewhere, people were keeping blogs and messaging online in the hope that they'd be heard and believed. In the meantime, we had: *Innocent obedience versus guilty dis-*

obedience to God. Why did this happen? Another's hand-writing, scrawled and nowhere near as neat as the others, answered above it: *You should ask: Why were we born into this?* That one seemed the saddest. Permanent marker on a glass window, there until broken or worn away with time. Or cleaned?

The words rattled around my head as I walked, overriding everything else, even a sharp *CRACK!* that echoed through the streets, and then another. Rifle fire. Close or far, it was hard to tell. At that moment, it didn't matter.

Even though I'd seen it on video, heard about it, in the flesh, St. Patrick's Cathedral on Fifth Avenue surprised me. The gothic building, all marble and stained glass and spires, was largely unharmed, just a little stonework crumbling at one front corner and, as I knew from Bob's footage, a hole somewhere in the roof.

I'd just take a quick look. I had to see the missile for myself. I had to see what had done all this damage to my friends, to everything here. I stood at the steps and hesitated. Then I climbed them, slowly, my legs suddenly tired. My limbs were weary of carrying so much around—so much guilt, so much fury.

The main doors were ajar, ash and snow piled up against them. The door hinges squeaked and I had to push with my shoulder and all my weight. The interior of the cathedral was lit by a dull blue light from the windows. On the floor, I noticed the glint of little golden coins. I picked one up. It was a holy medal, the picture of a winged man and the inscription: "Saint Michael Pray for Us." I wanted to hold it but my damaged left hand could not close to make a fist, and in my right I held the loaded Glock pistol. I didn't know how many bullets I had left but there were enough for any eventuality—any more than a few Chasers or attackers and I would be done for, anyway. I pocketed the coin, as if for luck.

Deeper within the church, the shadows were darker. I rummaged in my pack for my wind-up flashlight, but when I found it I discovered that, last time I used it, I hadn't folded the little plastic handle back in place and it had snapped off. I tried the switch; it was totally out of juice. *Damn.* I went through the smaller pockets, looking for—*yes, a lighter.* But its flame did little to light the way.

I inched forward, along the space between the banks of pews—an avenue of solace. Candle stands were dotted around the perimeter of the cathedral. I stopped to light three little white candles to carry as a torch. Remembering those times my dad and I had gone to church, I imagined who these candles might represent. I lit a fourth, for Caleb. No. I decided that the fourth was for that Chaser I dispatched. As long as Caleb was alive, he still had hope in this world. I left them there to flicker against the gloom. We all burn, eventually, all of us.

I took another candle and held it at arm's length, as I continued up the nave, my feet unsteady on the debris-strewn floor, towards the pulpit, the sole representative of a congregation of one. I could see the hole in the ceiling, nearly perfectly round, smaller than I'd expected, like that manhole in the street I'd climbed out of on the first day of this new earth. Light gray sky shone through, just like that day.

It was impossible to forget that Mephistopheles was just beneath me, ever present if I fell. He was there if I went down through the ground, never to return. He was always in every next step, waiting in the wings. But his nemesis, his rival, was here too and, looking ahead, my eyes focused on the cross before me, at the body of the man worshiped by so many of the people who had flocked here in safer times.

And there, by his feet, was what I'd seen in Bob's footage. Among the shattered timber and tiles, the unexploded missile lay bare. I shielded the candle's flame with my other hand, placing it between the missile and the warm light, and leaned closer. Brushed steel, no marking to give away the identity of its creator.

I knelt down, closer still: long pearl-strands of glass balls, deep-red colored marbles, exactly as Bob had captured on film. My mind worked overtime. Each ball must contain the contagion. Was it a liquid that turned to vapor when it met heat? Here before me, waiting to be released, was a fresh batch that could turn other survivors into the bloodthirsty Chasers, simply by being too close when the contagion reached the critical temperature . . .

Reeling, I felt myself break out in a sweat. What could I do? It was a massive responsibility. In a movie, there would be some clever way to defuse the bomb, to neutralize it, but I hadn't a clue how to do that.

I checked the illuminated dials on my watch—aware that I was on borrowed time. I turned—and tripped sideways, catching myself on a pew. To my right— rolling across the ground towards the missile—a lit candle.

I dived for it. Missed it.

I scrambled onto my hands and knees, crawled after it and lunged forward . . .

And blew it out.

I ran flat out, fast as I could, up Fifth Avenue.

What had possessed me to put my life in danger like that? To throw away all those days of caution? Going in there was stupid, but maybe I'd had to see it for myself. I'd been drawn to it. Maybe churches have that power over everyone, no matter what you believe. When the consumer gods are no longer talking—the billboards smashed, the adverts streaked with soot and water—maybe we have to listen to whoever is left. Or was I simply being pulled to join the others—not the religious, but the damned?

There was something exhilarating about surrender, about giving in to a force that was so determined to claim you. It was even more powerful than the instinct to survive. And why not let it take you away, spare yourself the effort of clinging on, of forging ahead? So much easier to let go . . .

But I kept on going, I kept running. The habit was too deeply entrenched in me now to do otherwise. And no longer did I worry about snow-covered holes in the road collapsing beneath me and swallowing me whole. I forgot about familiar dangers. I got to 56th. It was because I rushed, because I didn't bother to worry about my safety, that I let it happen. I was caught by surprise—didn't see or hear the attack coming.

20

Strong hands were pinning me down, then closing around my neck so tightly that I struggled for breath. A heavy, strong person, on me. His breath, fetid with old blood. I put my arms inside his and brought them out wide with all my strength. His grip loosened. I rolled and pushed him off but he was too quick—he was at me again, rolling me over to face him. He was clawing at me with disgusting blackened hands. I punched at him, twisted my body under his weight and wriggled to get away. He reached after me and bashed my head against the ground.

I flailed out with an elbow, felt it connect and I was free.

On my feet, I pulled the lids of my left eye apart with my fingers. The eye was okay, just stuck shut with blood; the stitches above my eyebrow must have opened up. I carefully touched the back of my head. There was a large wet lump. My fingers came away red.

He was on his feet and rushed me.

I sidestepped and connected an uppercut to his jaw as he shot past. He faltered, righted himself, and then I hit him in the sternum with everything I had. He doubled over on the ground; I kicked him and he fell on his side.

Up Fifth Avenue, another Chaser was running towards us.

Shit.

I ran away, eastwards on 56th.

Over my shoulder I saw that my attacker was back on his feet. Behind him, not one but four other Chasers arrived.

I could hear them running as I crossed Madison. It was impassable here to the north, forcing me another block away from my friends at the zoo.

I took Park Avenue and ran north. I knew the Chasers were still behind me. The streets were familiar, but that didn't make it any easier to decide what to do. I just knew I couldn't lead them to the zoo.

Ahead was 57th Street. Caleb's bookstore was at that intersection. It was secure, at least. Maybe I could hide without being noticed, let them run on by . . .

I dropped the steel bar into the brackets, locking the bookstore's doors behind me. It was near pitch dark in here. Caleb had blacked out all the windows, leaving small peepholes at eye level, with black sheets of paper taped over them like porthole covers. I tried to be still and listen; all seemed silent. Slowly, my eyes adjusted to the room. The sports gear strewn everywhere, the neat stacks of books, the whiteboard with the big scrawled note I'd left for Caleb last time I was here. Everything was as I'd last seen it, four days ago, although the carpet was wet and spongy underfoot.

The silence lasted a couple of minutes. While I wasn't eager to look outside, I had to know if the coast was clear. I lifted a corner of the paper covering the view-hole.

The Chasers had stopped in the intersection. I watched them as they slowly moved across the road, looking around the wrecked Citibank building, checking behind smashed cars, searching the snow for footprints. Maybe tracks left by someone else would send them down a wrong path, away from me. It was something to hope for.

I checked my watch: the minutes were slipping past. I took another glance outside. *There!* Across Park Avenue, the Chasers were backtracking. It started to snow, a light dusting. I didn't have time for a waiting game, but neither could I simply head out there and shoot my way clear. I doubted the snow would cover my tracks anytime soon.

I used the lighter to find my way around the ground floor of the bookstore as best I could. I couldn't recall if Caleb had any other weapons apart from the shotgun he'd had with him that last night. I couldn't see much of any use, though I found a skateboard helmet, which I tried on, but it only served to further aggravate the lump at the back of my head.

There was a shuffling sound outside. I moved to the side windows, peered under the flap. They were headed down the street, farther along East 57th. My heart raced as I watched them. *Please go, please don't come back.*

When I couldn't see them anymore I waited two more minutes, then went over to the doors. I lifted the bar—

Cold air rushed in. There was nothing outside except the falling snow. I pulled the doors shut behind me, ran across the street. The pistol was in my hands, but I was otherwise unburdened. At peace. A deadline ticking, but I was back on track now.

I took one final look back at the bookstore, and thought I saw a flash of movement in an upstairs window. My first, obvious thought was: *Caleb.* Had he been watching me? Why didn't he come down and attack me? I'd warned the people at Chelsea Piers that he might attack them, but in the back of my mind I suspected that I would be his number one enemy, that the contagion would have poisoned our friendship. Maybe it would be a point of pride for him to kill me—or if not pride, then whatever instinct motivated the Chasers. They *were* still human . . .

I considered the possibility—tentatively—that some part of the old Caleb remained and he might still respond to the bonds of friendship, that he had stayed out of the way just now, allowing me time and space to collect my thoughts and, most important, not alerting the other Chasers to my presence. A conflict of loyalties for him, an act of protection, perhaps even forgiveness. It was something to hold on to, at least.

But no reason to linger. I turned for Fifth Avenue—and stopped dead still. The Chaser I'd fought with moments ago had reemerged from an apartment across the intersection. There was nothing Caleb could have done for me, even if he wanted to. The Chaser saw me. I did what I'd been doing for near-on three weeks. Maybe the only thing I could still do. I ran.

21

I ran flat out up Fifth Avenue, all the Chasers now behind me—but thankfully, there was no sign of Caleb. I ran until a stitch threatened to burst open my side, but at last my goal was in sight: Central Park Zoo.

Inside the park, a couple of flights of steps down from street level, was a regal-looking building. The green copper sign at the top of the steps was reassuringly intact: "To the Zoo and Cafeteria." I followed them down, and ran around the side of the building where another sign directed me to "New York State Arsenal, Erected 1848."

I tossed my backpack over a tall metal fence, heaved myself up and over it, and landed heavily on the other side. There were several other brick structures behind this imposing building, covered and semi-covered walkways linking them, a big pool in the center. Another door led to the cafeteria.

"Rachel!" I yelled. "Felicity! Rachel!"

I looked everywhere, but there was no sign of life. Of course, I hadn't expected them to be keeping watch by the windows the whole time. They had things to do: routines, both their own and the animals'. But that was the weird thing: there were no sounds at all. Not a single bark or yelp or a scurrying of feet. Too quiet . . . I checked the ground beneath my feet. No footprints. So what the hell was going on? *Don't panic,* I thought, the silence all around me deafening.

If Rach and Felicity didn't appear I could climb the fence, using the side of the big brick building. I could haul myself over as I'd done before, but right now, with my banged-up knee and my aching head and hand, it seemed too big a task—

There was movement from around the side of the building. I waited, holding my breath, hopeful and fearful at the same time.

"Jesse!" Felicity said, a mixture of surprise and delight. She ran to me.

"Quick!" I yelled, heaving in a breath. "Let me in!"

"I don't have keys!"

"The back gate—tell Rachel to meet me there!"

I ran from her, past the outbuildings, the café, the parking lot, through the line of trees near East Drive, and skirted the back wall until I came to the steel fence set into the high masonry.

"Rachel!" I yelled. Again, not as loud this time, "Rach!"

Then I saw her running towards me.

"I'm here!" She reached the gate and fumbled with her keys, finally unlocking it. I fell through the gate and she slammed it shut and locked it behind me. "Chasers," I said, as she helped me to my feet. "Four of them. Come on, quick, we don't have much time!"

We crouched hidden in the cafeteria, catching our rapid, steaming breaths.

"This is crazy," Felicity said, getting to her feet and pacing the room. "We can't put our lives on hold. I thought the whole point was to leave the zoo, not lock ourselves in."

"They'll be out there," I replied. "They were right on me, and they're getting better at tracking prey." I didn't have much of a sightline here but I could see the side gate.

"Maybe they found a better meal," Rachel said, attempting a smile.

Felicity asked, "What did you find, Jesse?"

I took the can of Coke that Rachel offered me. "Thanks. I *found* them—the group, down at Chelsea Piers." I had a sip and put the drink down.

They looked at me expectantly.

"And what?" Felicity asked. "Are they—"

"There are about forty of them," I said. "And they've found a way *out*—we can get out of Manhattan!"

"Where?" Felicity asked, animated by the news.

"Through an access point to a big water tunnel, up near the reservoir in the park here."

"And?" Rachel asked. She looked a bit numb, detached.

It was clear that she could read me, that there was a big part of the puzzle still to place.

"They'll be there in"—I checked my watch—"right on three hours."

Felicity let out a funny little squeal of excitement and hugged me.

"Rach?" I said. She was looking off into middle distance, maybe weighing up the pros and cons.

"Look, I'm sorry it's worked out this way, having to move so fast, but they're our best chance of—"

"There's still a lot to do," said Rachel, writing on a pad as she spoke. "We need to be methodical with our time left." She handed Felicity and me a handwritten list each. "My pack's ready; do your own, then get onto that."

With those instructions, she ran from the room. Just like that. I slipped off my pack and put it next to hers, which was overstuffed with clothes and a few items of food. I went to the window and looked around at the empty zoo grounds. I caught a glimpse of Rachel walking fast with buckets of feed. It reminded me of when I'd first helped her, just a few days ago.

Felicity put an arm around me. I spoke quietly. "What's with her?"

"She doesn't mean it," Felicity said, "being mean, I mean. She's been worried about you, and been itching to leave here, should you show up like this."

"Has she been okay, since the snow leopards?"

"No," Felicity said, setting a pot of water onto the wood fire to make us all a hot drink. "That was it for her, the final straw. She's been . . . she's been really angry, until you showed just now." She paused, then went about packing her backpack. "So Caleb was right: there was a group at Chelsea Piers."

"Yep. Over forty of them, like I said: men, women, teens and kids, most fit and healthy."

"What are they like?"

"Mix of locals and tourists, from L.A. to Russia to Brazil, but they're all there and working together," I said, taking over the making of some coffee. The heat of the fire was bright against my frozen face. "It was good to see a scene like that, seemed almost—"

"Normal?"

I frowned remembering what Paige had said. *Normal is a cycle on a washing machine.* But I guessed they were normal if you could describe people with divisions and prejudices as normal. Humans attacking one another, that was probably normal, too. It didn't get us anywhere, though. I stood by the window. I decided to tell Felicity the truth, whatever her reaction might be.

"They're a unit now—well, they were when I met them, too, but they were divided over leaving."

"Because they had a comfortable setup?"

"Pretty much; that and the dangers of the unknown and wanting to wait for help."

"Jesse," she said, zipping up her pack. She came

over, stood close to me by the window, rested her head on my shoulder and hugged her arms around me. "You really think this group has what it takes to get out, to survive?"

We watched Rachel walk out through the court, past the central pool of the sea lions and towards the building that housed the Tropical Zone. I liked that she looked so measured, so methodical. Time to go help. I filled the thermos.

"What choice have we got?" I said. "It's them and now or never."

"There's always choice, you've told me that."

I put on my pack and slung it with Rachel's over my shoulder.

"I'm not so sure about that anymore."

We walked downstairs.

"And you're having second thoughts?"

"No, it's just hitting me now, the finality of it: I'm leaving."

22

There were two entry points into the arsenal building: the doors that faced the fenced zoo grounds, which we used all the time, and a set of doors facing Fifth Avenue, which I'd barricaded a few days ago after an attempted break-in from Chasers. I considered dismantling the stacked barricade and building a slide-down brace like Caleb's setup, using timber from old doorjambs to slot across the doors and brace into position. Instead I added more furniture to the stockade. Wind whistled in behind the big bookcase that was pressed against the broken glass of the doors, but it'd do—much better than it was before.

After that, I carted water to the animals from the empty polar-bear pool. I checked off my list, making sure I didn't miss any of the little critters. I found Felicity and Rachel feeding the penguins.

"We'll have to let all the animals loose," Rachel said.

"You can't be seri—" I began, but the look on her face silenced me.

Felicity shook her head, as if to say, *Don't go there. We've been through it all already. You're not helping.*

Rachel shrugged. "Surely you factored that into your plan, Jesse? I mean, it's not as if we can take them with us—what, like a circus procession?"

"No, but I thought—" I stopped. What did I think? I knew that so long as the animals were alive, Rachel's link to the zoo would be intact. Of course she couldn't leave them here caged. Perhaps I hadn't really accounted for what this part of Rachel's journey would cost. I guess that had been one of my big mistakes all along: not thinking about the *journey*. It wasn't like stepping-stones, easily moving from one stage to the next. This was hopscotch, and the stakes were life or death. Each step changed you, changed how you saw the future. That was how my whole notion of home had collapsed. It had changed so much it was unrecognizable.

Rachel could see that I was stumped. But she didn't have it in her to be angry at me for long. Perhaps she was just too tired.

"We have to let them go, let them fend for themselves," she said. "It's what happens in nature." She looked around her, aware of the irony that you couldn't describe the world around us as natural anymore. Felicity went over to her, tried to offer reassurance, but Rachel shrugged away the gesture. "It's okay." I think she meant that the animals here, like us, were about to take the next step into the unknown.

I was silent. I watched Rachel as she looked around

the grounds. As if in acknowledgment of their fate, the animals began to gently bleat and groan and mew. For a moment, she and Felicity exchanged some low murmuring words—private, comforting.

I could tell that Felicity had been a sounding board for her, that Rachel hadn't had to torture herself with thoughts of guilt and regret in my absence. The girls seemed to be getting on well still, but I wouldn't push it by asking about it. Whatever way they'd found to endure the last few days was their own success, their own business, and separate from what the three of us had been through. Maybe it wasn't my place to intrude on that, or to try to share it.

I didn't want to be left out completely, so I said, "So, how do we do this?"

Rachel smiled. "You remember your crash course in looking after animals from before? You know where everyone is, what their temperaments are like."

I nodded. "I'll do my best."

"Okay. The best thing to do is open all their enclosures and prop the doors tight so they don't close," she said, "and then—stand back. Don't confuse them. Don't try to influence them. Just let them do their thing."

"Simple, hey?" I said.

Felicity smiled weakly, as if she knew what Rachel's response would be.

I should have expected Rachel's frown. "Not really. Not simple at all. Letting go is never simple."

I knew the truth of that.

Rachel turned to me, put a hand on my shoulder—different from the way Paige would have done it, but still good. Nice. "You can't help him, Jesse."

"I guess."

"He's lost, Jesse. There's nothing you can do."

I nodded. Knew I had to believe that, but I wanted otherwise, wanted hope. In the end, I knew he was as helpless as these animals.

"I'm serious." She grabbed hold of me, not out of anger but to make a point of me listening to her. "You'll screw yourself up if you think otherwise, okay?"

"I know," I replied, as she let me go and touched my face. "I know. It's just I didn't think it'd be this hard saying good-bye to this city . . ."

We stood out on the back step of the building facing the frozen zoo grounds.

Felicity said, "My brother, in the air force—"

"Yeah. He's a medic, right?"

"Yep. When he went to Iraq, it was the hardest good-bye I ever had. But you know what, it turned out okay—we all got through it, together. What's meant to happen will happen. Just go with it."

"Okay," I said.

Felicity nodded. "Some of these guys will be okay. They've got instincts. They're adaptable." She was talking to Rachel now, back to their private shared moment. "Are you sure you can do this?"

"Yeah—" Rachel pulled the two of us into a hug. "I'm at peace with leaving them, and it's probably a good thing that I don't have time to think it through, or else I might hesitate too long . . ."

"Come on," Felicity said, as we set about our solemn task—almost as solemn as the snow-leopard funeral. "We'll do this and leave them to it."

That moment said so much about what we'd experienced together as friends. It was as hard for me to leave Caleb behind as it was for Rachel to turn her back on her animals. Well, add that to the issues I'd need to talk to a shrink about someday—and that was something I still looked forward to, if that day ever came. Imagine it—sitting in a doctor's office, talking about these problems I currently faced. It'd mean I was on the other side of this, yeah? That'd be a great day. A perfect day.

23

Afterwards, I went upstairs and sat on the edge of my makeshift bed. I looked at my well-used map of Manhattan, marked up with all the little places where I thought Caleb may be, along with routes that I'd been on highlighted. So much walking, I could see now, although mostly around Midtown and up to here.

I ejected the clip from the Glock and checked how many rounds I had: eight. I hoped that would be enough. Felicity made a pot of porridge over the fire. I knew we had to eat, because who knew when our next meal would be? We had no idea how long it would take to get through the tunnel, assuming we made it that far into Central Park.

The small second-story room in the arsenal building was a warm and cozy squeeze. Just a few days ago, when I'd met Rachel and she'd been all alone here, it'd been empty, with only the barest of necessities stacked on a table and shelf, a few neat stacks and tubs of wood for the fire, a few buckets of fresh water.

Now there were clothes aplenty, food for a few weeks, three beds and bedding, and all those little things that we seemed to add along the way: books, lamps, games, trinkets, iPods—all that looted stuff added to all that we were leaving behind.

"Is the generator still in the vet rooms?" I asked as I zipped up my backpack.

"Of course," Rachel said, putting a bucket of water to heat on the fire. "Why?"

"I can run it till we leave, charge up all our—"

"I wouldn't bother," Rachel said. The last of her tasks done, she took off her jacket and sweater. Her socks looked soaked through, her jeans and T-shirt were caked in mud, and her face and hair slick with sweat and grime. There was no doubt that she and Felicity had been working hard to keep things ticking over these past days. "We've got a few flashlights charged. They'll do."

"Okay," I said, settling another small split log on the coals. I felt sick and numb, waiting like this, like lining up on the starting blocks. To get our last bits together, to make our way through the park . . . the apprehension, the anticipation, swirled in my stomach like a swarm of butterflies. "Hey, what's the collective noun for butterflies?"

Rachel smiled. "You know, I'm not sure. A swarm?"

"A flight?" I said.

"A flutter," Felicity said. "Or . . . a kaleidoscope."

"That's cool," Rachel said, taking the bucket off the

fire. She soaped up with a washcloth and started washing herself. "What made you ask that?"

"Nothin' . . . just a few nerves."

She nodded.

"I know what you'd call a group of wankers," I said. "A handful."

"HARR!" Rachel erupted in laughter as I'd never heard her before.

"Genius," Felicity said, stirring the porridge. "One of my friends who worked on Wall Street used to always joke about 'recessionitis'—like bronchitis that's chronic, but it can take months and years to go away."

"Nice," Rachel said, drying off and changing into fresh clothes. "My dad used to joke that he needed 'approval from corporate,' i.e. my mom, to buy anything."

The girls laughed. I stared out into the dull gray zoo grounds.

"Jesse?" Rachel looked up at me as Felicity passed her a steaming bowl of porridge. "What is it?"

"Nothing," I said, a little too quickly.

I watched the fire crackle and spit. I had a memory of my parents in that image, of a night when we'd slept in a place in the country, down by the coast, in tents. I'd left my tent flap open and saw my dad put a log on the fire and then he sat there, with my mom, an arm around her shoulder; I watched them sit there until I fell asleep. That's my favorite memory of my mom and dad being together.

Outside, the afternoon sky was turning dark and

light snow began its drift upon us. "Come on," Rachel said. "We've got twenty minutes, let's get moving."

Rachel put on layers of thermal clothing while Felicity poured us coffees. Warmed by the hot drinks, we checked our provisions for the last time. Then we shouldered our packs. "The reservoir will be full of Chasers," I warned. "No hesitating out there: just *run*, don't *stop*, don't look *back*."

"Yes, I know it, but they're the easy-to-deal-with kind," Felicity said.

"What about the ones coming towards us now?" said Rachel.

For an instant, I thought she was teasing. But the jokes were over for the day. I went to the window and looked out at the zoo grounds. Initially, all was peaceful. I was about to laugh it off when we heard noises. I hadn't reached the rear doors when the familiar Chaser appeared, followed by others, approaching the side gates.

I ran towards the veterinary rooms. Inside, I grabbed a gas can from next to the generator and shook it. Only about a third full, but it would have to do. I locked the rear door behind me, came out through the open storeroom, and unscrewed the cap on the gas can. Through the windows I saw the Chasers had got into the arsenal building and were now banging at the back door.

I pulled off my backpack, took the lighter from the

side pocket, and splashed the gasoline around the door. I kicked over the can at the steps to let the last of the liquid dribble out.

"It's okay," said Rachel, giving me permission to do what had to be done. "There's nothing left I need. The animals are gone."

So I lit the match, dropped it on the ground and stood well back.

"You two get going," I said, nodding urgently. "Go out the front way, it's safer."

If they argued, I didn't catch their words. *Whoosh!* Fire leapt up, spooking them, holding them at bay. I didn't want to destroy the zoo—I just wanted to put enough distance between us and the Chasers while I ran to the back gate.

To my relief, I could make out the forms of Rachel and Felicity running up ahead on the East Drive, crossing 79th Street. The girls were moving faster than I was. With every few strides I took, I was falling another second behind. They rounded a bend and I lost them again. I gritted through the pain and ran hard. At least all was clear behind me.

There was a noise overhead, a mechanical sound, and I ducked as it appeared to be closing in—but I couldn't see anything. An aircraft? Another minute of running flat out and it was there again. Getting louder too. I remembered seeing on Bob's little screen some footage of the initial attack: several shots of blurry high-speed missiles streaming into Manhattan neighborhoods, their red-hot plumes streaking across the winter's sky.

A louder noise rumbled and shook my bones as it passed—right above me! The whine of an engine screeched overhead. It was a sound I'd heard before. To confirm my suspicion, I looked up through the intertwined branches of the bare trees and saw it. A drone aircraft, the same kind that had attacked the soldiers' truck.

Its course meant it was headed to where my friends were headed . . .

I ran faster, giving it everything I had.

24

The bottom of Central Park's recreation reserve was a near-endless white blanket, easily the size of several football fields. It definitely was more vast than I'd given it credit for from up high in 30 Rock. I ran for the far northern tree line, where I was due to rendezvous with the group. Beyond that, another smaller park and then, over 86th, the reservoir and our way out of this city—so close.

I checked behind me. The Chasers were a way off but the distance between them and me was narrowing. I could outrun them. And maybe the size of our group might scare them off. The worst-case scenario would be we'd have to fight. I turned and checked again—still a way off, maybe even falling a little behind.

Yes!

I ran hard.

I was crash-tackled to the ground, a hard and terminal stop, like a truck had hit me. I got to my hands and knees, spluttered for breath, heaving. I was kicked in the ribs, knocked onto my side, winded. Above me, a boot came crashing down towards my head. I ducked aside but felt it graze my nose and tasted blood in an eruption of pain.

As the Chaser above me moved in for another attack, he came into focus.

I knew him.

"Caleb!" I yelled at him with everything I had. *"Caleb!"*

There was no recognition in his eyes. Had he stalked me from his bookstore?

"Caleb, no—"

My infected friend lunged at me, and I shuffled backwards in the snow, my backpack pulling me down. Before I could make another move he was on me. I went with his momentum and by shifting my weight sideways I flipped him over my leg. I got my arms out of the straps of my pack and felt instantly lighter. I stood as Caleb got to his feet, too. I wiped my bloody nose with the back of my hand.

"Caleb! It's me! Stop!"

His expression remained vacant, his gaze fixed on my streaming bloody nose. I had no idea if he recognized me or not, if he cared.

Over his shoulder I could see the other Chasers were only maybe sixty seconds away.

He made a move and so did I. I pulled the pistol from my coat pocket and brought it around to fire above him. Caleb smashed into me. The gun fired high into the air and fell from my grip into the snow.

"No, stop!"

All his weight crushed into my chest via his knees and I tried to wriggle free but it was useless; his strong hands pinned down both my wrists. His face closed onto mine and I lifted my head, quick as a flash: my forehead hit him squarely between the eyes and he rolled off me, hands at his face, stunned.

But not for long.

I rolled over and scrambled on hands and knees towards the pistol, a black angle in the ankle-deep snow. I reached out for it . . .

The weight of Caleb crashed into me again. We tumbled and rolled, then his hands found my neck and tightened, closing around my throat. He was squeezing hard, strangling me from behind.

I reached for the gun, my arms outstretched and my fingers flexing . . .

It was too far away, just beyond me.

I shook and squirmed and tried to wriggle free—

I gained a few inches' distance and I dragged him forward, my eyes watering. I was nearly out of breath but I kept pushing away from him and suddenly I felt his grip loosen.

My fingers clawed forward in the snow, digging and reaching, but it was still too far and my vision began . . . to . . . blur.

A quick gasp and I sucked in some air.

I lunged forward but he was right on me and pushed my face into the snow, drowning me . . .

I elbowed and squirmed with the last of my energy . . . When I knew I had no other choice, I went limp.

He let go, flipped me over onto my back. I waited less than a second.

I saw his surprise when I opened my eyes.

I reached up and clapped both my hands over his ears, hard. He reeled back. A tiny win, but the other Chasers were now upon us. As I moved for my gun, there was a noise—loud, mechanical—and a vehicle came into view.

The Ford pickup truck—Bob at the wheel—rumbled its way from the top of the reserve. The whole Chelsea Piers group came into view. Not a hundred yards away.

The Chasers held back, weighing up their situation.

"JESSE!" I heard Rachel yell out. "Jesse, over HERE!"

She was standing with Felicity at the opposite topmost corner of the reserve. Everyone was in their place but me.

Behind me, Caleb approached with care. There was no mistaking him. A predator with the desire to hunt, to kill, and no concern about his prey. Step by step, wary, but eyeing only me. Beyond him were more Chasers, holding at just twenty steps away. I looked back for the pistol, but stopped cold.

Again there was a noise in the air—ferocious, manmade, getting *really* loud, *really* fast.

The hairs on the back of my neck stood up and I prickled with sweat and nausea in anticipation.

THUMP, THUMP, THUMP. Louder than anything I'd ever heard before.

The Chasers reacted too; they started edging back. Caleb still had eyes only for me.

I scanned the white blanket but could no longer see the pistol in the deep powder snow, which was billowing around my ankles in a strong wind. I backed away from Caleb as he came closer. Beyond him, the empty gray Manhattan skyline, and that noise—no longer a deafening thump but a loud and constant whine and roar. The other Chasers neared, their fear appeased by the prospect of a feed in me. There were some familiar faces in their crazed stares, their haunted look so natural to me now.

"Caleb, don't *do* this!" I yelled at him, but he didn't register. He'd fully checked out.

The noise became brutal, unbearable, and the wind as strong as I'd known it. I had to slam my hands against my ears. Finally, even Caleb could do nothing but turn to look for the deafening source.

From the west, there was movement against the low dark clouds; by the time I'd processed what it was, they were practically on top of us. Aircraft. Dozens of them, planes and helicopters, even something that resembled a combination of both, coming in hard and fast from all points of the compass. All painted a dull military gray. Massive propellers chewed at the sky, ripping through the freezing winter air, the bigger crafts' blades tilting skyward on stubby wings. Each aircraft made a vertical landing on the massive rec reserve.

Whoever this was, an invasion or a helping hand, they had no regard for the infected. They started shooting: laser-like beams of machine-gun fire that tore into everyone out in the open. I had no choice but to stand there and take whatever was coming.

"No!" I pushed and shoved—Caleb was on me.

I looked up at his face. We'd talked and laughed—shared dreams and plans and confidences—and now this.

"Stop!" I punched him in the side of the head but he didn't seem to notice.

His arms were longer than mine and he was heavier and stronger than me; his hands again found my neck and took hold. He'd survived this long on the street, so he'd probably killed like this before.

I think I saw the sun come out, but it could have been my eyes playing tricks as I was choked. I'd imagined what this would be like—imagined it would be epic, brutal, the absolute end for one of us. I knew that, whatever the outcome, I would lose something, my life or part of myself. That it had to be at the hands of my friend seemed so unfair. I tasted blood in my throat and realized I couldn't fight it anymore. My hands went limp.

Caleb's grip tightened. I turned my head from him and saw groups of people, watching from the tree line. They were Chasers. A scant few had blood around their mouths: hunters. Most were the weak ones, but they watched just the same. A hundred of them, maybe, all up. Familiar faces. A boy, thin and tired. He looked from me to those around him.

I didn't fight. *This* Chaser was helping me: Caleb was sending me home. I tasted blood in my throat as it was being crushed. *This may be my last taste, my last breath. I'm going home . . .*

I am floating above the ground. I've dreamed of this, of flying through the city. I see the buildings as if I'm lying flat on my back and looking up, backstroking my way around, light as air, effortless, the feeling of any and all kind of possibility. It's cold.

I feel hands on me. I picture that image from one of Caleb's art books, that photo of a ceiling from the Sistine Chapel. I saw it with my grandmother six years ago. I feel time, I feel motion, and I feel cold. I am not alone, and I am not going home or anyplace I know. I fall.

I'm on the ground. I see faces. Expressions of concern. They look at me and I smile because I know where I am now. I am among friends. People. Chasers. All indistinguishable now, all little versions of reality, all offering different meanings of the word home, ready to take me.

I didn't hear the gunfire.

I felt the hands around my throat ease, then let go. Caleb was still on top of me. I could clearly see his face lit against the dull afternoon sky. He looked down at me and I'll never forget this: there was *recog-*

nition. He knew who I was and in that final moment he *smiled.* Then, he was gone.

"When I die," he said, "I want to go on living."
I nodded.
"You will."
He smiled.
"Take my journals. Keep them. No one can kill my words. You understand?"
We sat there. The gray-blue sky. The bare branches of the trees. The brief flight of a seagull. The breeze. I was wondering what to say to him. I had nothing . . .

When I woke, I was lying on my side in the snow, my cheek pressing into the cold, a film of frost over my damaged eyebrow. I could see soldiers running from the aircraft. Shooting. I remembered: *They killed that group of Chasers.* I heard screaming too—yelling, but also stern commands. I felt hands on me and I looked up, to a vision I had never expected to see again.

Rachel, Felicity, Paige, and Bob. They were all there, by my side. I wanted a moment alone with them, to check that each and every one of them was real, was okay. I wanted them to be friends and to support one another. I wanted them to tell me we were safe, that it was all over. But there was no time. Almost straightaway, the soldiers came up to them. My hearing was coming back online but I couldn't make out what they were saying.

I didn't need to. I could tell that things had been worked out: we were alive, and the soldiers were not going to shoot us. I saw Bob there, the camera in his hands, filming away. Next to me, no sign of Caleb. At last, had he got what he'd asked for? Or had he vanished, alone out there for one final act? I sucked at the cold air, smaller and smaller gasps, until my breathing stopped.

25

I drifted in and out of consciousness . . . I was aware of it, but whether this was the end or another part of something, I had no idea. It was nice, to go with it, to float away . . .

Summer heat, blue sky, the smell of cut grass—I am home. Laughs, jeers, hanging with mates . . . I remember this. It's the school holidays, before I enter my final year of high school. Homework and classes are still a few weeks away, so it's nothing but eating and sleeping and mucking about.

The sound of the basketball off the backboard. The cry for the rebound. Legs a blur as I'm knocked over—the slide long, the heat of the polished court on the way through. Playing this game today I'm in a combat situation. My mind is functioning but I'm not thinking in a normal way. My memory isn't even working normally. I'm so hyped up, amped. My field of view changed. My capabilities changed. I am under the influence of adrenaline. Makes you respond quickly, think faster. Speed is key.

I get to my feet. Time is called and we have a drink.

The day is hot. Flies circle around me, silently flying back and forth on never-tired wings. Dust blows into the school gym through the open doors from the field that hasn't seen rain in about fifteen years. Least there's a breeze. Without that, this place would be unbearable.

We're playing a group of big guys. Leading their team is the older brother of the guy I'd beaten for the one spot to represent Australia at a UN camp. This other guy really wanted to go but I beat him. I reckon the poor guy probably spent all year on his essay. I'd written mine in an afternoon. Now his brother is out for revenge.

Back out on the court. Looks are exchanged. They think they've got us licked.

Yesterday's friendly shooting of hoops is now a fight to use this court. If we don't beat these guys, we're off this court for good. We lose, I'll get pushed around some more. They say this school wasn't always like this.

When the school year starts, I'll have to perform—to get as good a score as I can with subjects I don't really like and teachers I don't rate. I'll be at the bottom. My locker will get smashed to shit and pissed in. My bag will be stolen. I'll be pushed around.

On my feet I run to intercept the pass—too slow.

The guy blows by the big brother for a left-handed lay-up. He hits a thirty-footer. They're four up. Seconds to go.

"Jesse!" my captain yells. He's grabbed a rebound and uses his elbows to get defenders off him. Big Brother—BB, he likes to be called—fouls him hard and I stare at him. BB

makes a twenty-foot turnaround. One of his guys gets through me, I catch up but I'm blocked out, he pump-fakes three times and uses the glass for a deuce. It's shifting back down our end. Captain advances on a three on two and dunks it. We're on it again as our captain drives the lane and dishes towards me at the last minute for a bucket. They all stare at me and time stands still as I go for the long shot, knowing if I miss I'll embarrass us all.

I'm on the ground and our ref for the morning calls time and there's shouting going on.

"Jesse, you alive?" my captain says, grinning down at me.

I nod. My vision clears. I taste blood.

I ask, "What happened?"

"That idiot clocked you on the way through," he says, helping me up. I'm wobbly on my feet. I hear the other team laughing. Our captain says something, Big Brother replies with a gesture and:

"You got a big mouth, fat kid."

"I'll take this idiot down," Cap says, but I hold him back by his shirt.

"You can't take a crap," I say, my voice different through my swollen lip. "Come on, we can't lose this. Let him worry about putting me down again if that's all he wants to do. Let's win the game."

We start up.

Cap's our power forward. He dribbles beautifully up the court—I lead our teammates in clearing out the key. Defensively, BB's guys are solid with their blocks. Just as fast as us but with extra bulk. I try to get past BB but their de-

fense is stifling. I pass under, it's rebounded, and I pass backwards. Happens like this again until it's deflected out. I check the ball in. Cap dribbles up top, makes a one-eighty spin with the ball, and pulls up for a three-pointer. BB reads it perfectly and rejects it.

I'm there and I snatch the ball off the fast break and pass behind to Cap—who dunks it! Everybody courtside goes nuts. BB walks to the sideline, ignoring all the fist-bumps being offered. He talks to his team. Seems everyone of them is now riveted on me. Great.

Back in play I take a pass and turn to—BB puts his elbow into my face, sending me to the court's floor. My world spins.

Cap yells: "Come on, ref! He's throwin' elbows—call offense!"

Time is called. For keeps this time. We lose by a point.

"That's crap," I say to my mates as they help me up.

"You guys wanna play on?" ref asks. I see Cap's holding a swollen eye of his own, can't think straight. Ref turns to the other team, busy high-fiving one another. "Extra time?"

"Bullshit," BB says. "He was movin' his feet!"

Ref looks to Cap who shrugs—neither of them exactly sure what happened. Maybe Cap doesn't want to escalate things, or drag out our humiliation or injuries.

I sure know what happened. If innocence were a commodity BB and his young brother would be bankrupt.

I shoot a look to the other team. I shout for all to hear:

"Shut up and listen. I got a new bet. If you're game."

BB stares at me.

"Call it scores are level," I say. "To find a winner we take turns to shoot until we miss, twice. In a row or not, you miss two shots, you lose. Losers, their whole crews, never come back. Never."

"Okay then Jesse, for the year," he says. "We win, you grab your goons here and find a different place to run.

Not just for this summer . . . forever. You win, and we don't come back. No hitching, no fighting, here in front of everyone."

Cap steps forward.

"Nah, not you," BB says. "Him."

Of course, he points at me. My head spins and I swallow some blood. One of BB's other guys is rubbing his elbow and points it at me, looking down his forearm like a sight, as if to say he'd purposefully lined me up.

"Okay," I say. "Let's do this."

BB pulls off his T-shirt—he's huge and ripped.

"Piece of cake," I lisp, blood dribbling to the ground.

I go first. Easy shot, nothin' but net.

BB scores easy. Like this for a bit.

"Yeah jeah!" Cap calls. "Nice shot!"

I step up for the fifth shot. My side watches intently. No pressure. I'll be outta here in a few days anyway.

I miss.

Their team exalts, their crowd cheers. I suck it up. We make our own mistakes. Own it. Don't miss again.

BB steps up and sinks another. Too easy—he's a full head taller than me and built of solid confidence.

I take a breath. I can feel my heart racing. I settle it, take *a moment, a third and forth bounce. An easy hoop ahead. Like the world after a storm, I am cleansed, feeling anew. I release.*

Score.

BB steps up, one bounce—misses.

My boys hoot. Our injured bench give the thumbs-up.

BB pops the ball into my chest, nearly blows me off my feet.

"Don't miss."

I don't.

His ball. I bounce it into him. Smile. He bounces three times. Watching the hoop. He bounces again, another three times. Shoots.

Scores.

My eye is swollen, my lip cut.

Sweaty as hell. BB calls his little brother over. He stands under the hoop, putting me off. I take a drink of water, spit out more blood, look at my bitter opponent, and say nothing.

Look at his face, his shit-eating grin. He starts to say something—

I turn and walk away.

He yells at my back: "Yeah? That it?"

I turn back. Take the shot. Off the backboard, around the rim, and through. Score.

There's not a sound.

I say, "Get ready to get off our court."

BB quickly pivots past me, dunks it, and yells as he hangs on the rim. The crowd cheers. Mucking around. He knows he has to line up from the foul line.

He stands there and bounces.

He and I lock eyes, a look exceeding competitive boundary. A look filled with rage. One down each. Could be his last shot, he could make it and then it could be mine. Make no mistake. I feel sick. My final bellyache.

He bounces twice. Jumps for the shot.

In.

Me.

When you're afraid to miss you miss because you're afraid.

I go for the shot—but I'm blocked out of it.

Caleb is there: he intercepts and is now bouncing the ball.

"What," he says, "think you can just leave me behind?"

26

When I came to, I was on a stretcher, in a medical tent set up in a rapidly expanding tent city, ringed by aircraft coming and going. I saw plenty of commotion through the clear plastic sides. Hundreds of people dressed in uniforms ran around with weapons and equipment.

Medical staff rushed about just as urgently. The doctors and medical staff who attended me were gentle. They took some blood samples, then cut off my clothes and wrapped me in a silver foil wrap and a blanket. My bandages were changed and an IV inserted in my arm. I wanted to protest, say how Paige had chosen those clothes for me. Ask how the others were. How Caleb was.

Soldiers rolled out wire fences along the perimeter of the rec reserve. Others were setting up machine-gun posts. They're settling on this little piece of Manhattan, I thought; protecting it. Why? Then what would happen? Would they spread out, radiate out into the city, offering whatever help they can provide? Too little, too late . . .

My friends were there, all lined up and talking to soldiers.

A few of the soldiers had video cameras, and a couple of people who were dressed in civilian gear looked like news crews setting up. A set of TV screens was banked up on a table in the corner of the tent with a large satellite dish outside all of it, connected via thick cables to a big green generator.

First, I heard the voice of a female news reporter: "It's been twenty-one days since the attack, and here in Manhattan we are at a quarantine zone being set up near ground zero . . ."

In a moment I saw their news feed via a screen. I stared at the passive faces talking to cameras. Logos of news agencies and networks flashed up. All making their claim as newsbreakers, as if this were just like any other disaster.

My awareness still flickered in and out—for how long exactly, I don't know, but judging by the fading daylight it may have been a couple hours. It was easy to imagine what used to be here, around me, in this mess. What was charred and burned in this landscape. What the contents of this dust and debris and ruin used to be. Billions of cells of human beings, reduced to another form of carbon, and here we were living and breathing it.

A nurse patched up my face. She poked and prodded, fixed up the cut above my brow, which was now
swollen and throbbing. She'd taken my blood earlier
and handled everything with care. Every now and
then I heard gunfire, the sharp crack-crack-crack of
military assault rifles.

"What is this?" I asked her.

She looked down at me. The tent was vibrating as
aircraft took off or landed.

"What's what?"

"This . . ." I said, with a wave of my hand. "All
this, all these aircraft and equipment—who are you?"

"We're US military," she said with a small smile.
"We're here to help."

I smiled, she smiled back, but the unspoken question hung heavily between us. Where the hell had
they been all this time?

"Why—what took you so long?"

"Quarantine," she said, revealing only what she had
been instructed to say. "We had to wait this long."

She spoke as efficiently as she worked, and eased
some wadding up my nostrils, holding it in place with
tape.

It was the first time I'd heard the word. The way
she said it, so neutrally, denied it of the significance I
knew it must really have. "Quarantine?"

"Exclusion zone, containment."

"So you've been out there watching what's going
on in here all this time . . ."

She didn't reply, but it wasn't as if I needed clarification. The explanation was obvious. It had been all around me for the whole time. All those aircraft I'd seen or heard these last three weeks, that was them, watching, waiting.

"Here, I'll help you sit up," she said, and helped me prop myself up against some air-inflated pillows. She put a little device in my hand, a button linked to the IV. "Press that if you feel like there's too much pain."

A big group of soldiers walked past the tent, moving out. There must have been at least sixty of them. A few were dressed in some kind of shiny space suits.

Then I saw a spark. A flame. What I had guessed were air tanks on the soldiers' backs were in fact some kind of flamethrower—hot jets of fire that would squirt across streets, burning cars and bodies. A cleanup crew. They would light fires, burn wrecked cars. I had half a thought that the flames might start it all again—it might ignite some spore of the contagion, or explode some hidden missile that hadn't yet gone off . . .

"No—" I shuddered.

"It's all right," she said, calm as ever. She tried on a reassuring smile, made some notes on my chart. There seemed to be a lot for her to write. I guessed it was my story, at least her interpretation of it. From time to time she looked across briefly, inspecting the television screen. She nodded to me, as if saying I should look at it. All the answers I needed were being revealed—at least, all the answers I was going to get.

On the screen was an image of the US president standing in front of the cameras, surrounded by generals. I thought back. Wasn't he in New York when this happened? Did that mean he got out—or was this file footage?

I tried another question. "Who was responsible for the attack? You must know that by now."

"Depends who you believe," she said.

I couldn't read the news ticker from this distance but I thought it said something like, *". . . the EU, China and Russia are cooperating . . . ,"* then the screen changed to footage showing a sign that read: *USAM-RIID Headquarters.*

"Please, tell me," I said. "Australia. It's my home. Is it okay?"

She looked out the door as the news crew ran by, animated. The screen now showed a live feed from a helicopter flying over Manhattan. Streams of people, many thousands, streaming out of buildings and other refuge areas and heading towards Central Park. Survivors.

I imagined standing in that street, still, among this mass of survivors that I'd barely seen any hint of before, a crowd that'd be all laughs and cheers and tears as they streamed past me. Firefighters, cops, suits, kids, homeless, all walks of life beaming with hope at the arrival of help, waving up at the passing chopper. Who they became in those three weeks had been pushed back in their psyche, now they were all New Yorkers again.

"Please, my home—"

Someone was tapping on the side of the tent and I looked across and saw my friends standing there. Paige waved, Bob gave me a thumbs-up. I smiled at them, then turned back to the nurse. She was looking south to the view of the aircraft and Manhattan skyline. I could just make out the top of 30 Rock.

She turned to me and I had a million other questions to ask her, but above all I wanted to know about home. Her eyes found mine. There was a moment of sadness in them, but no answers. Maybe holding onto the truth was her way of protecting herself. Maybe she thought she was protecting me.

27

"Jesse!" Felicity rushed into the tent, Rachel not far behind her, the two of them dressed in blue jumpsuits and wearing surgical masks. "You okay?

"I think so," I said.

Rachel gave me a hug. "We've just passed quarantine, been scrubbed to within an inch of our lives," she said. "They're making sure we're all okay before moving us out of the city."

"Where?"

"Haven't said, somewhere upstate."

"They've set up a perimeter around Central Park," Felicity added. "They're just using this place as a base to venture out into the city from, until they treat all the survivors that they can, and then they'll deal with the infected."

"What about the group from Chelsea Piers?"

"They're all in one of the camps here," Felicity said. "They're going to be airlifted out to an off-site quarantine base upstate."

"How are they reacting?"

"They're all fine," Felicity said, then with a smile: "A cute little Valley Girl named Paige said, *like,* to say *hello,* and tell you they're all, *like, okay . . .*"

I laughed at her mimicry of Valley-speak. "What about you guys?"

"They said I could go back to the zoo," Rachel said.

"It didn't burn to the ground?" I said, surprised and delighted.

"No, you're a crappy arsonist, Jesse," Rachel said, and smiled. "But it did the trick. It got us away from the Chasers."

"But what use is it?" Felicity asked. "Now that the animals are gone."

Rachel shrugged. "That's what I told them, but they've already set up security there. It's as safe a place as any."

"*Will* you go back?" I asked.

Rachel shook her head. "An emergency team of relief workers from the Fish and Wildlife Service will arrive tomorrow to take over, care for whatever animals are left. Then I'll head west."

"Your family?"

She nodded. "I just spoke to my mom on the phone. The west coast is fine."

A doctor in military fatigues entered. He was young, and had a friendly face that looked somehow familiar.

"Jesse," Felicity said. "This is my brother, Paul."

"Heard a lot about you," Paul said, shaking my hand. He inspected my medical chart. "All looks good. You'll be able to check out of this bunk in the morning."

"Good," I replied. "Can't wait to get out of here. I'm so glad we're all okay. It's amazing, really. There's just . . . one thing—"

"Caleb?" Felicity said, but she shook her head, and turned to Rachel.

"He ran off," Rachel said. "I saw him make the tree line to the east before the aircraft touched down."

"How did he look?" Should I tell Felicity's brother how I'd *seen* Caleb become infected?

"It was hard to tell," Rachel replied.

"He'll be fine, for now," Paul replied. "But he won't have long out there in the city."

I looked at him, trying to figure out what he'd said—was he saying that as a medic, or did he know more about what was going on here?

"What—what is it?" I asked, thinking maybe I'd missed some pertinent point. I pushed the morphine button.

"They've got cleanup squads gearing up to go out tonight," Paul said.

"Cleanup—for what?"

"Probably be out there doing it each night for a while," he said. "At least until this quarantine zone is closed and the curfew in the city's lifted."

"What's that?" I asked, sitting up further. "I—I don't get it, like cleaning up the mess so they can drive down the streets?"

Paul shook his head. "They're going out to 'clean up the streets'—that's their term, not mine. It means they'll kill all the aggressive infected—"

"They can't do that!"

"I don't like it any more than you," he said.

"Can't—can't they do it some other way?"

He didn't answer, but Rachel asked: "How many do they figure are infected like that?"

"They've put the number at one or two percent."

"Of the infected population?"

"Yep."

"And they'll just *kill* them?" I felt like I was going to explode, a hot rush of frustration flaring up my neck. "They can't *stun* them or *catch* them?"

"It's how they're doing it," Paul said, checking around as if wary about being overheard. "Damn criminal if you ask me."

"Criminal?" I said. "It's *insane*! I mean, they're fellow *people*, Americans, tourists . . ."

It was clear Paul and the others felt exactly the same; I could not take my anger out on them.

"Why are they doing this by night?" Rachel asked, her voice quiet and matter-of-fact.

Paul motioned at the news crews over his shoulder, still broadcasting outside and interviewing some of the survivors. Tom and Paige were talking to them, Audrey was nodding silently, all of them dressed the same as my friends here, in the quarantine garb.

"So that they and their choppers don't get footage of it. The city's a no-fly zone by night."

"So, it's just so that they can do their dirty business in secret?"

Paul nodded.

"And what will they do with the other infected?" Rachel asked. "All the thousands out there now, being corralled—"

"They'll be fine."

"How do you know that?" I asked him.

"Because this virus wears off."

What did he just say? But there was no mistake. "Wears off?!"

"The worst of it has subsided," Paul said, looking around the tent. "Slowly, the infected's faculties return and, as they do, we can treat the docile ones. Frostbite, exposure, malnutrition, physical injuries— the list goes on. It's going to be an epic task."

"And—what?" I said. "The others are seen as too hard to treat?"

"They're too hard to handle and since there's no cure—"

"So just kill them?"

"There's no improvement in them," Paul said. "It doesn't wear itself off like with the others, there's really little we could do, even if we rounded them up someplace."

"So they're doomed to die or be killed?" Felicity asked.

"Looks that way."

"So, these teams . . ." I paused, thinking it through,

"they're going out when it's dark, when the media helicopters are not there, to kill the worst of them, and there's *nothing* we can do to stop them?"

Paul said, "Right now there's no choice—"

"There's always choice."

"Jesse, I know what you're saying, but in this case—"

"There *has* to be a way."

"They have to do it this way to move fast, so that they can process more survivors and more of the other infected, like you guys and like all those thousands gathered around here."

"You can't save them all, so why bother even trying?"

"We have to triage this," Paul said. "This—they've got contingencies for situations like this, protocols that they follow. It sucks, and I'm sorry about your friend. God knows, we've all got friends out there."

We were all silent for a bit. Around us, the noise seemed to grow louder: the hum of the generators powering the medical and heating and lighting equipment, the constant comings and goings of the aircraft, the babble of hundreds of people as they passed.

"How many are there like us?" Felicity asked. "Out there in the city?"

"Estimates are around half a million."

"Half a million?" It was much more than I would have guessed, but then New York was a giant city. I'd barely got to scrape the surface of it before the attack happened. Maybe it was a good thing I didn't have a proper sense of scale, otherwise I might have decided escape was just too big a challenge. I took in the statistic once again, tallied it with my own experience. It still didn't seem real. "I've been here alone—I've seen hardly any evidence of survivors, let alone half a million."

"We know that most people sheltered, in their apartments or in mass refuges," he explained. "New Yorkers have had it drummed into them for years, everyone is pretty much prepared, with their duct tape and ration boxes and whatnot. Hell, I just heard that Madison Square Garden alone has been packed with close on fifty thousand, Empire State had another twenty—"

The thought of so many people out there in these streets was . . . incredible. I'd felt so alone at times in this city that was teeming with people—people just like me, thousands of them who'd probably felt as alone or even more so than me.

"Have you heard anything about Australia?"

"I don't know," he replied. "I've not heard anything about it, but London, Paris, Moscow, Shanghai, Rio—quarantines all around the world are being lifted as we speak, so it's too soon to tell the full extent of what's happened."

My head spun from the enormity of it, but also at what he'd said: if it were global like that, what chance did little defenseless Australia have?

"How will you get all these people out?" I asked.

They all looked at me. "The survivors—how will they know that it's okay to come out now?"

"They've got armored convoys going out from tomorrow morning, pushing routes clear so we can start busing people out to the north. They're giving instructions by megaphone and dumping info flyers, and we've just got radio broadcasts back up and running today, with TV following in a few days once the power's back on. Medevacs are already running, as you can hear."

As if on cue, a helicopter buzzed deafeningly overhead.

"Paul, you said before that there was no choice," I said. "About these guys who are going out to kill the worst of the Chasers—the infected."

He nodded.

"I have a friend out there."

"I know. I'm sorry—"

"No, you don't understand," I said, sitting up in bed, the drip line in my arm pinching as I moved. I looked from him to Rachel and Felicity. "There's *another* way, *another* choice, I know it."

"I'm sorry, this is their doctrine."

I tried one last time. "Well, what if they *do* get better?"

"They don't—"

"Or what if there is a cure?"

"Jesse, this has been analyzed in labs—hell, the US-AMRIID team here has worked around the clock."

USAMRIID . . . "I *met* some of those guys!"

"They came in here to test you?" Paul asked.

"No," I said. "They came into Manhattan, *days* ago."

"No," Paul said. "Those here today are the first responders on the ground."

"I saw them too!" Felicity said to her brother, her voice rapid and tinged with excitement. "I was with Jesse; they had their ID on a container in their military truck, and we saw them getting attacked by a UAV."

Paul looked taken aback. "When was this?"

"A few days ago."

He looked spaced out, computing all this.

"Tell me *everything*."

"You don't think that's weird, that there was a group of US soldiers here on the streets, transporting an unexploded missile out of Manhattan, *attacked* by their own aircraft?"

"We don't know that for sure."

"It was, Paul, it was a US aircraft, you know it," Felicity said. "Attacked by our *own* people, like they weren't meant to be here, doing whatever they were doing."

Her brother was clearly struggling to take in the possibility.

"What do you think they were doing?" I asked him.

"The USAMRIID?" Paul said.

I nodded.

"I don't know," he said, looking out the tent's clear side panel.

"What if they were getting rid of evidence?" It was one of the ideas I'd tossed around with Bob and Daniel.

"What?"

"That they were here to get that missile and take it away—to hide it—because the missile or the contagion was US in origin."

"Something like that has happened before," Rachel said. "With the anthrax attacks. Apparently, they were said to be perpetrated by US armed forces—"

Paul shook his head. "I doubt it. I mean, why not just destroy it?"

I told him about what happened when the aircraft struck the truck, about Caleb being so close . . .

"Are you sure it was a missile from this attack that they had in the back of their truck?" Paul asked.

"Yes, absolutely sure," I said. "This guy, Starkey, told me that."

"Starkey?" Paul said, shocked, as if the name meant something to him. "I've met him—he was a colonel in the USAMRIID, a brilliant specialist in infectious diseases. You're sure that was his name?"

"Yes."

"Describe him."

I did. The more detail I provided, the more ill Paul looked. He shook his head. "It can't be!"

"Why?"

"Because he's dead."

"I know," I said quietly, trying to show a little bit of respect. "The last time I saw him he was dying." He'd been bleeding badly, blood pumping from his stomach, but even as he lay there in agony, he'd tried to help by warning me about the danger of the missile.

Finally, Paul looked freaked. "We were told today that he and his team were killed a few days back, in a lab incident at Fort Detrick."

"Who told you that?" Felicity asked.

"Our CO," he said. "The general in charge of this quarantine op."

"Why would he lie?"

He shook his head, looked around, as worried as I'd ever seen anyone. "I don't know."

"It was a US aircraft that swooped down and destroyed the trucks and killed them," I said. "It was, wasn't it?"

Paul nodded. "We're the only ones that have aircraft like those you described."

"Killing their own and covering it up," Rachel said. "In case anyone is wondering, that there's another example of why I prefer animals over humans."

Felicity put a hand around Rachel's shoulders.

"This virus," Paul said, "it only lasts a certain time in the air and on the ground. Call it an hour, max. We wanted to send crews looking for samples but it was deemed that we were far too late—that this contagion is dead, the risk looking under rocks too high."

"Their doctrine," I said.

Paul nodded.

"But what?" Felicity asked.

"If we had a sample of it from ground zero, we

could try to work up an antidote." Paul looked at me. "Jesse?"

"I can do better than that."

The girls looked at me, too.

"I can show you where an unexploded missile is," I said, the image of the explosion and subsequent infection of my friend Caleb as fresh in my mind as that missile at St. Pat's.

"Where?"

I shook my head. "No. I'll show you."

The two girls looked worried but I could tell that Paul was wavering. I pulled the IV needle from my arm.

28

It was pitch dark when we prepared to leave the quarantine zone.

"Jesse, this is a situation where darkness will not be our friend," Paul said.

The three of us—Paul, Felicity and I—were dressed in black camouflage outfits complete with bullet-proof vests and helmets.

"Do we really need helmets?" Felicity asked.

Her brother was firm. "If you're coming, it's my rules."

"I'm not letting you out of my sight," she said, and the pair of them hugged.

"Most serious injuries on the battlefield are insults to the head and are easily preventable by these," he replied, rapping his knuckles on the Kevlar shell atop his head. "Of course, you could stay here."

She punched him in the arm, their argument about that long over and won by her.

Rachel hugged me. She was still dressed in the

quarantine outfit, although she now had a coat on over it. "Be safe, be quick."

I nodded, and we slipped out the side gate by the zoo's arsenal building, itself as defiant a survivor as I'd ever seen. The soldiers in the upstairs windows didn't wave or seem to take notice, such was their ambivalence to us sneaking out—but their boss, a gruff army major, was a friend of Paul's, and after a heated conversation he'd arranged our covert leave pass via his security post here. Rachel locked the gate, the major by her side.

We raced up the stairs to Fifth Avenue. I had to be quick and be safe—Caleb's life depended on me getting back with a sample. I knew the dangers that lay ahead: the so-called cleanup squads tasked with shooting any threat on sight; the Chasers out for their nightly hunt; getting the sample of the contagion from that missile and taking it back to the quarantine zone. They were only a tad less scary than the other thing working against us: time.

Silenced weapons of silent killers. We watched from a first-floor window of a Fifth Avenue store. Paul took the night-vision goggles from the clip on his helmet and passed them to me. As I looked through them, the green-hued world around me came alive.

Below our position, a group of Chasers walked the street, wary. They were headed south, and walking right into an ambush: eight figures were crouched, hidden from the Chasers' view, some behind cars and others behind the columns of a building opposite. I could see their night-vision goggles, their raised weapons.

The silenced submachine guns spat jets of bright flaring flames. I passed back the goggles, rubbing my eyes. At least a dozen long tongues of death as the soldiers did their devil's dance in the street, wiping out the group of Chasers. I'd never felt so ashamed.

Fifteen minutes later we emerged once more onto the street.

We were silent, the three of us, Paul with an assault rifle ready and night-vision to guide him. It had become windy.

"They're gone," he said, scanning the street up and down.

I led the way to the south. We walked in silence, stopping every few yards to be still and listen, never moving until Paul said so.

In my pocket I carried the only vestige of my former outfit, the tiny little holy medal I'd found in the cathedral. I rubbed it between my thumb and fingers, waited while Paul watched from another window at the front of a store. It smelled of death inside here, and I didn't have the stomach to search around for the source.

"They're close," he whispered.

Felicity looked at me, the shine of the moonlight

reflected in her eyes. The three of us headed deeper into the store, behind an aisle unit that had tipped over and spilled its contents, the mess a pattern of repeated destruction that I'd seen so often.

"You know those patterns that repeat themselves?"

"What?"

"Like, the pattern is the same no matter what the size, you know . . . I've been wondering about it my whole time in New York."

Felicity shook her head, looked at me like I was nuts.

"Fractals," Paul whispered. "Like the Mandelbrot set."

"Yeah, thanks," I said, and he went back to keeping lookout, peering through the shelves from where we sat crouched in the dark recess of the store.

"You should have stayed back there," I whispered to Felicity. "This isn't safe."

She hugged me, said close into my ear: "I don't ever want to be left behind again."

An hour later we waited. Twice Paul went up to the front of the store to watch and listen, twice he came back, convinced it was too dangerous for us to leave. Paul headed out—waited outside by a smashed taxi in front of the store. No sign of a cleanup squad of killers, nor Chasers. Not a sound here except for the constant drum of military aircraft echoing through the streets. He called us out. The three of us by the cab, watching, waiting, listening.

"Can we go?" Felicity asked.

"I think so," he said. "Jesse?"

"I'll lead," I said.

He reached for his night-vision goggles and passed them to me but I declined them. "I'm used to the dark," I said. "And these streets. Come on, it's not far."

"One more block south, at the intersection," I said.

"Rockefeller Center?"

"St. Pat's."

We squatted down behind a burned-out van. A flash of light in the sky illuminated the charred metal panels.

"What was that?" Felicity asked.

She was answered by a dull rumble, followed almost instantly later by heavily falling snow.

"Thunder snow," Paul said.

"What?" I asked.

Another flash. I could make out the lightning this time, then the deep rumble of thunder closely followed. Snow fell in a thick heavy blanket.

"It happens sometimes," he said. "A thunderstorm, but it snows instead of raining—it means the weather system is unstable, and it's gonna be a rough night."

A RIP-CRACK right above us, so loud it made the three of us jump and Felicity screamed; the lightning hit at the same moment.

"How long will this last?"

"Maybe an hour," he said. "Reckon the snow'll keep coming, though."

As well as the bolt of lightning there was a low, drawn-out rumble.

"One more block?" I said.

The two of them were huddled close to me.

"I'll lead this time," he said, his night-vision remaining on his head, useless amid the flashing light-show above. "We won't be able to hear much, but they won't have their night-vision on either—may even force them inside a building for a break."

St. Patrick's Cathedral was a solid slab of dark and cold, intermittently broken by blades of colored light shooting through the stained glass.

"Where?" he asked.

"Down by the pulpit," I replied.

We moved quickly—there was no time to light candles but the interior was made less sinister by the flashlight mounted on the end of Paul's assault rifle, the piercing beam reaching into the darkest shadows.

"Wait here," he said. He took off his backpack and passed us each a clunky black object made of plastic and rubber. "And put these on."

The three of us pulled up our gas masks. Paul did up our straps and checked the seals. He gave me a thumbs-up, passed me his assault rifle, and went the last few paces with the light of a glowstick to guide him.

Another flash, followed several seconds later by

thunder—the noise seemed to enter through the hole in the ceiling and reverberate around the cavernous space.

"Is it blowing over us?" Felicity asked, her voice shrouded in mystery via the gas mask.

"Yeah." We watched as Paul reached the spot where the missile was and started to take samples. I saw him hunched over, working by the dull light. Another flash of light, this time it took nearly ten seconds for the thunder to sound.

"Do you really think that so many people could have sheltered in places like this?" Felicity asked me. "Half a million?"

"We did," I said, thinking back to when I'd first seen Felicity: it was on a tiny video screen, the diary-type entry she'd made in her parents' apartment, and that's where I'd viewed it, only a day after she'd left; I'd managed to stay at 30 Rock twelve whole days before properly venturing out. "We lasted it out for nearly two weeks."

We watched Paul place a small black box into his pack, then head over.

"True," she said. "But—but we've seen such little evidence of survivors, certainly not on the scale that my brother said they expect to receive in quarantine over the next few days."

"Maybe most of them gathered in big spaces," I said. "Refuge areas." Hell, I'd thought about that enough times, that possibility. It would drive me crazy to think about it now.

Paul joined us; he took off his mask and we followed suit. "Got it—let's move."

All his samples were in bagged containers and secured in his padded backpack. I could feel them moving close behind me as we ran to the first corner north. How could I convince them to leave me out here? I wanted to go and find Caleb, trap him, put him somewhere secure until this antidote was ready. If my home was gone, I needed to do this—I had to *right* something. I had to *do* something.

We stopped at 52nd Street.

The thunder was fainter but there were still deep flashes of lightning somewhere high above in dark clouds as the heavens continued to fall in sheets of snow.

From the cover of a building's corner, Paul surveyed our path north.

As Felicity and I huddled a few feet behind him, I noticed bumps in the snow: frozen bodies, real life snowmen and -women.

"Felicity," I said, close to her ear. She turned. "I can't—"

"Now we head back, careful as we can, same drill," Paul said as he came over to us. "Quiet, wary, no risks."

Another big flash of lightning lit the scene around us for a couple of seconds, clear as day.

To the west on 52nd, a group of Chasers. Beyond them, a cleanup squad.

In that moment, all hell broke loose.

29

Behind us, the screams of Chasers and the thudding of bullets were punctuated by a long, low growl of thunder.

We ran. Paul was faster than me, and Felicity nearly kept pace.

Glass shattered around us and bullets zapped.

Paul skidded to a halt behind the fallen facade of a building across the street and we crashed in behind him. Another stream of bullets tore at us, sending up plumes of concrete dust from our barricade. I pointed across the street and we kept ground-close as we ran to more cover.

"Can't you call them off?" Felicity screamed as we raced behind some massive granite columns, hugging the facade of the building as we headed south.

"No!" he answered. "They're on their own comms gear."

"Surely you can—"

"Flic, we can't risk it," he said to her. "There's something going on here, some kind of cover-up, way back up to the general. We have to get these samples back, so I can head straight to the USAM-RIID team to work up the antidote, got it?"

She nodded.

My thoughts of Caleb remained, but I had to see these guys back first. I knew these streets. Another flash of lightning, another volley of gunfire punctured the scene around us. Paul turned and fired a stream from his rifle—perhaps giving our pursuers something to think about: *We're not an easy target, we're not Chasers, we're technically on the same side*—well, maybe.

The cleanup crew was having none of it: the windows above us blasted out, raining safety glass.

"We have to get off the streets!" I yelled into Paul's ear above the thunder.

The storm was moving away with a drawn-out moment of final torment.

"Come!" I replied, leading the way along a dark street. Felicity dragged behind me as I pulled her along by her hand, keeping close to the buildings on our left and using the shattered remains of vehicles on the street to provide cover.

We crossed Madison Avenue.

Another flash.

A yell, close by.

Paul.

"No!" Felicity screamed.

We helped him to his feet. I dragged him as well as I could—he'd been shot in the thigh. We rounded the corner onto Madison and I guided them down into a subway station below us, the curtain of heavy snow-fall left behind.

I switched on the flashlight on the end of Paul's assault rifle. Down we went, silent but for Paul's whimpering.

He fell to the ground in a heap; both Felicity and I were spent.

"We . . . have . . . to keep moving," Paul said, propping himself up with the aid of a turnstile.

In one hand I held out Paul's rifle; I hefted his arm around my shoulder and we entered the main hall of the station.

Hundreds of faces, staring back at the light.

Chasers—the docile kind—watched us wide-eyed. A gaunt sea of pale expressionless faces.

"Jesse?"

"It's okay," I said, and we pushed and shoved our way through the mass towards the platform. Some moaned and groaned, some were clearly close to death, and the smell . . . "This way."

The subway tunnel seemed intact as far as the flashlight would penetrate, knee-deep water obscuring the floor beneath our feet. The Chasers watched us at first, then soon went back to their grazing. At the end of the platform we found an open janitor's closet-cum–staff bathroom.

"This will do," I said. I managed to put the broken door back in place and latch it shut behind us. We sat Paul down, and he cracked another couple of glow-sticks. He pulled bandages from his pack, a kit with syringes and vials, and a tourniquet.

"Is it—"

"I'll be fine," he said to his sister.

I shone the flashlight on the wound as he wrapped it up.

"Okay," he said. Felicity helped him elevate the limb onto a bucket as he eased himself down. "I'm done."

"Can you move on it?" I asked.

He winced in pain. "No, not all the way back to the quarantine zone—"

"Paul—"

"Not with them out there, Flic."

"He's right," I said. "It'll get us all killed."

"So . . . what do we do?"

"Can you wait for first light?" I asked. "Once those cleanup guys are gone?"

He looked up at us and his sister whimpered because we both knew his answer: he couldn't make it, and those samples had to get back to the QZ fast.

"I'll go."

They weren't listening, they were arguing. Arguments, even now, after all this—only human nature, after all. I switched off the flashlight and the sudden darkness startled them, extinguishing their conversation. I switched it on, and they looked almost guilty.

"Nice one, Jesse," said Paul, with a smile.

"I said I'll go," I repeated. "Paul, I'll take your pack

back to the quarantine zone, via the zoo entry. I'll send help back here for you."

Paul nodded.

"No," Felicity said. "We can't split up. We can do this: Paul, the three of us can—"

"No, he's right," Paul said. "He can send help, a medevac. I'll be good for a few hours, but hurry, and tell them my injury."

"But—"

"Flic, I know these streets, I can do this," I said. I picked up Paul's backpack and put it over my shoulders. I passed him his assault rifle but he refused it until I insisted. In exchange, he passed me his pistol, which I tucked into the side of my belt. "I'll be as quick as I can. Don't move, but if you have to for some reason, I'll come back here with help and stay here until you can somehow make it back to this spot."

"We're not goin' anywhere," Paul said. He handed me his night-vision goggles, which I clipped onto my helmet. Felicity hugged me and saw me to the door.

"Help will be here soon."

Outside the snow continued to fall, the lightning infrequent and the thunder now just a far-off rumble. No sign of those soldiers. I ran north fast, stopping at corners, weighing up the right moment to dash across the streets as lightning flared, saturating the night-vision.

I was at 57th and Madison. With so much snowfall,

there were no footprints. It was eerie looking through these things with their otherworldly greenish tint.

The zoo was about eight blocks away to the north-west. I could make it within half an hour at this cautious run-stop-check-run pace, and have the major at the arsenal building send a med team back within an hour. So many times had I passed this intersection, the waypoint between the zoo and Caleb's bookstore just a block to the east. I had to see. Five minutes, tops. A look and I'd done what I could, right?

The pack on my back was light but I felt its weight with every step; failure to return was not an option, not at all. The thought of what was on my back, that it could somehow be synthesized into an antidote to the worst of this, saving Caleb and countless others like him, was spurring me on as much as the need to send help back to those two below the street. I took off at a sprint.

No . . .

The bookstore was burned out, still smoldering and aflame in places. Most of its windows had shattered and glass crunched on the snow underfoot. On the single piece of glass that remained in the door was a painted symbol that fluoresced in the artificial glow of my night-vision goggles. The work of the so-called cleanup crew, no doubt. What did that symbol mean for Caleb? I wondered.

There was a noise behind me.

I turned, pulled my pistol and fired in one motion.

A man. I'd fired high. It spooked him; he ran. I recognized the gait, the clothing, the quick glimpse before he'd turned. Caleb.

He was ten paces away when I set off at a flat-out run after him. He must have feared those soldiers, for good reason, and figured that I, in this outfit, was one of them returning to finish the job.

I tripped because the goggles limited my view of my feet. I flipped them up and ran, momentarily blind in the near-complete darkness of the snow-filled night. My eyes slowly adjusted to the gloom. He was just ahead of me. I could hear him huffing and puffing and panting his way forward—he'd grown weak or tired.

"Caleb!" I yelled.

I stopped and from the silence and stillness I guessed that he must have too. I walked slowly forward, expecting to see him materialize before me, stepping through the dense curtain of snow. He was not there.

Lightning shattered the thick blur in front of me. In the murk, I saw the figure of my friend creeping through the broken doors of a department store. I paused, just content to watch him, as if he were an ordinary guy, picking his way over rocks at the beach or something, nothing in mind but the need to explore. But no matter how long I stayed there I couldn't guarantee reclaiming the humanity in my friend—it may have been lost forever.

So I got to my feet and followed him.

★ ★ ★

Inside was a darkness so complete that I couldn't make out where the labyrinth of aisles and counters began and ended. I'd only ventured a little way in but as I retreated to the safety of the front doors I tripped over abandoned bags and baskets, empty cash registers, and endless power cords snaking into a jumble of wires.

"Caleb?" I called, quietly. "Caleb—"

There was a shuffle to my right, then a crash. I smiled. I couldn't see Caleb yet but I saw the racks of clothes he'd disturbed tumble to the mess on the floor. I flipped down the night-vision and the world around me became that now-familiar green-tinted dream. I scanned the space around me—nothing but more racks and displays of now-defunct luxuries.

I retreated to the doors, my boots making loud footfalls. My heart raced, not at the possibility that Caleb might surprise me, but at the thought that he wouldn't. Maybe I really *had* lost him this time.

More illumination from the wild sky outside lit my path as I crunched my way across, past the windows, to the far side of the store. I passed a storeroom behind a big sales counter. Inside it was dark, of course, but it appeared to be empty. It would do.

I made a lap of the store, keeping the front doors in view so I wouldn't lose my bearings, taking care to make as little noise as possible. I just had a feeling that he must be here, somewhere. I kept a steady watch, and listened carefully. And then—

Breathing. Soft, rhythmic, human. Right next to me.

I squeezed the pistol tight in my right hand, then, with my left, reached out into a forest of hanging clothes—and pulled Caleb out.

He fell onto me, pushing down to try to knock me backwards. His hands clawed at me. His fetid breath burned hot against my face. I swung my right arm out so the pistol clocked him on the side of the head, and kept swinging. He rolled off me in a heap. I knelt up, ready to hammer again at him if I needed to. But he seemed subdued. Not out cold, but that only happened in movies. He was dazed but full of tremors.

I returned the gun to my belt, and dragged him across the tiled floor by his ankles. He moaned slightly as his face and skin connected with bits of broken debris. At the storeroom I pushed him inside as far as I could. Quickly, I backed out and pushed some steel clothes racks between the doors and the sales counter, to stop them from opening outwards. He was imprisoned there, my friend; a fact which only I knew.

He rattled the doors, in anger or desperation—both, I guess.

"Caleb, this is for your own good!" I told him, trying to reassure us both.

There was more noise from the storeroom in response. I rifled among the looted drawers of the counter, and found a big marker pen. In big, bold letters I wrote across the doors: MY INFECTED FRIEND CALEB IS IN HERE—PLEASE GIVE

ANTIDOTE. I signed my name, as if to reinforce my pledge and promise.

Now, I had to get back to the quarantine zone.

Back at Fifth Avenue, I ran north. So close. The weather had eased, and the streets looked marginally less angry than before. From the shadows of an apartment block awning, I scanned the road ahead. The coast seemed to be clear.

I didn't see or hear a movement. The next thing I knew, I was shot in the chest.

30

The force of the gunshots on my bulletproof vest threw me back against the wall of the apartment block. Slowly, I slid my way down to the pavement.

I fought to breathe, clutching my chest with my left hand, while my right pulled the pistol from my belt. I crawled back to the shelter of the awning, and tried to gauge where my attacker was. I struggled not to cough as my lungs fought for air. Even with Paul's night-vision, I could see nothing more than an empty street—the familiar wasteland of wrecked vehicles and three weeks' worth of packed snow.

I thought of Paul. How long would he last, bleeding back there? Four hours? I hadn't debated the point because of Felicity. But it was obvious he needed help ASAP. Hell, none of us had any time to spare.

In front of me a wrecked car offered another bank of protection. I managed to clamber onto the bonnet, checking to my left and right. I held on, fighting pain, for as long as I could manage. Just when I was about to lose my grip and subside into the snow, I saw them.

Four armed men. Moving close to the ground, fast, down Fifth, to where I'd been shot. I could see my footprints snaking a clear path from them to me. I blasted a few rounds of the pistol straight up into the air. It wasn't much of a threat, I know, but it might have given them pause for thought. Maybe.

I ran the remaining distance to the zoo. In my mind's eye I would always picture my first impression of it—as a secure fortress among the ruined city buildings. I had feared its destruction and wanted to be reassured by its survival. In the dark I could just see the outline of the arsenal building. I was about to descend the steps when the stone pillar with the sign attached suddenly disintegrated into a hundred shards. The side of my face stung and burned.

More gunfire rang out. And then I was shot again, this time in the back.

At the bottom of the stairs I was flat on my face. I pushed up, my world spinning from the impact of the hard, icy ground. I could make out soldiers up there in the windows of the zoo's main building.

"Don't shoot!" I screamed at them. *"Don't shoooot!"*

I tried to get up but couldn't. I panicked about my pack, about the contagious samples being ruptured, but realized it was too late either way. *Keep going, get it back, send help to your friends . . .*

No bullets came my way, but flashlight beams shone down on me. I wriggled out of my pack. I looked up at them.

"I'm back—it's Jesse! I have the sample—please, help me! Rachel!"

The flashlight beams didn't waver.

"Help me!"

Shuffling, up at street level. I heard talking from the building, then—gunfire.

A spray of bullets, loud and unsilenced, blasted at someone up on Fifth Avenue—at whoever had shot me in the back moments earlier.

There was noise at the doors to the arsenal building. I looked up the entry stairs: in the light of more flashlights I saw Rachel burst out, that friendly army major beside her. They raced down to help me.

"Jesse!" Rachel yelled, "Jesse!"

I told her and the soldier about Felicity and Paul, gave them the address of the subway station, and the army major got onto his radio to dispatch a medevac convoy.

I passed Rachel the backpack.

"Get this to them, the samples are in there."

"We will, come on," she said, "I'll help you up."

"Rach, I can't. I can't move."

I looked down and so did she: there was a dark pool of blood in my gut—the bullet had blown clear through from my back. She collapsed to the ground next to me.

"Oh, Jesse," she said, cradling my head on her leg, my face in her hands, "Jesse, hold on, you'll be okay."

By now there were a dozen soldiers around us,

there to help. One started to uncover and assess my wound.

"Caleb," I said. "I . . . locked him, in a storeroom, of a store—" I felt faint. I told her where to find him. "Make sure they get him . . . treated."

She nodded. I was aware of hands pushing a hard stretcher under me. I couldn't feel my legs.

"Jesse . . ."

31

ave speaks.
Why can't you leave?
I speak.
Because I have what I need here.
What do you need? Anna asks.
You, I think, but don't say. I need you. And you. And you . . .
But—
Now I have new friends. Rachel. Felicity. Paige. Saw Caleb again too—
He'd asked you to kill him.
I couldn't.
But you could leave us.
You were already dead.
There's silence for a beat.
And what, you just replace us, that easy?
I shake my head.
None of this has been easy. What was I supposed to do? Rot with them? Wait for death to claim me, not put up a fight, not bother about survival? I say:

If I could have gone your path, I probably would have.

Cop-out.

No, it's not, really . . . I want to smack Dave, but hey . . .

Well, you didn't follow us. You're there, living in my stead.

Is that it? I ask him. Do I have to live for you now?

Didn't you know? he says.

Don't listen, Mini says.

I wish I could hug her for it, hold her, my BFF and beyond.

Do what you have to do, she says. Live for yourself.

The other two are silent.

I don't say anything—I feel guilt, again, guilt, guilt, guilt. Maybe I shouldn't feel that way, maybe I should just succumb, join them, for that's the alternative.

I stand with Anna. The other two walk away, busy. She looks at me as I want her to. So compliant, in the little ways. She's sixteen like me and she'll stay that age in my mind forever: she will never fade, because I will not allow it; I will never forget. Her English accent, her beautiful Indian skin, that dark shiny hair, her long-eyelashed eyes and her lips—that bright red mouth, burned onto mine, forever.

Let me go, she says.

I did, I reply. You came back.

You brought me back.

How?

How should I know?

We had stood on the roof of the building at 30 Rock. Sixty-seven stories below, we'd kissed. That was over two weeks ago. In two minutes, I might be dead. Hell, maybe I already am, who's to say?

Anna asks: Why?

I don't know.

But you know?

Yeah.

Change it.

What?

Change it.

How?

Don't die.

It's that easy?

She doesn't answer.

I say: Forgive me if I don't believe you.

Yeah. Great. Do that.

What?

Be like that.

What?

I know? You left me, remember!

Did I?

I thought about it. Did she? Ultimately?

We stood at that intersection near Broadway. I was ready to run.

I take a final look at my friends. Anna is looking directly at me—has it always been that way? Her back to that familiar storefront. This is the place. This is where we say good-bye.

You sound sure of yourself, she says.

I'm remembering, I say.

Oh. Right.

Yeah.

Change it.

I can't.

Change it.

Change this?

Why not? It's your memory.

Why not? Because it made me who I am. Change this, those memories, what do I have left? What's the point of living if we just make it up?

Don't we? Make it up?

I suppose. But I don't want to change it, not this, not now. It brought me here.

Where? Where did it bring you?

I look around.

Here, I say. I'm at Central Park Zoo. I am asleep. In a minute, I may be dead, but my sleeping self does not know that. There are other figures in the room. Sleeping, under blankets, forms of life; love.

Look, Anna says. It could be us.

No, I reply. I can no longer see Anna. I hear her voice, I watch myself and the three other figures in the room sleep, knowing it was only once, so briefly, like that. I know this scene as clearly as I know anything. I am there.

Be careful, Anna says.

It hurts.

Everybody hurts. Just hold on.

To what?

We are on a subway, the last car. I see a fireball, in the tunnel behind us, chasing us. It's hot and bright and black. I am on my stomach, my world a mess around me. I close *my eyes. It's easier. I know what follows, what I'll see, and I don't want to see that again. I close my eyes and I wait. It's coming. It's hot as hell and it's bright as the dawning sun and I know now that I will never wake up. I am joining my friends.*

The final thing I hear is a voice, female, it could be my mother's, Anna's, Mini's, Rachel's, Felicity's, Paige's . . . but it's not. It's loud and it's close and I hear it again:

"Jesse?"

The nurse checked me over. Doctors hovered. I could see through the clear plastic wall. The soldiers heading out. The sun was setting and in the coming darkness I could see fire, the flames enormous, there was an explosion that shook the ground. The sounds of screaming and crashing and then everything went . . .

From hot to black.

I'd miss this place, the cold, the people, the peace and quiet. Back home, it would be hotter than I could remember and life would have a different rhythm. Here, my friends would remain, rebuilding and getting on with life, laughing and crying as their world was built again.

"Jesse?"

later . . .

"Jesse?"

I looked at the psychiatrist's clock. There were four in the room, so wherever the head-shrinker chose to look she could be sure of the kind of punctuality that probably mattered once. Outside it was dark, but the blinds were drawn, and the overhead light flickered for a moment, then burned steady. It had been almost an hour, so I was sure our time was about up. She'd listened, mainly, as I'd talked, but had followed that up for the past minute or so with silence as her note-taking caught up.

I'd been watching her write, lost in it, didn't notice she was trying to engage me in more conversation. "Sorry?"

"I said," she repeated, she didn't sound annoyed—more a professional coaxing—"that's quite a story."

I fingered the gauze above my eyebrow.

"Three friends who carried you through—"

"Then I let them go."

"Then you let go," she said. "Then you made three new friends—"

"And I had to leave them, to see what else was there."

"What happened to Felicity and her brother, Paul?"

"They're fine. They got helped out by a convoy not an hour later."

"And Caleb?"

I smiled. "They worked up the antidote and by the next night they were spraying the entire city with it. Caleb was where I'd left him, and they got him out. He's—he's doing okay, as well as any of them."

She sat silently, made a further short note in my file. The silence went on; clearly I was meant to fill it.

"What do you want me to tell you?" I asked. "That Caleb turning into a Chaser and disappearing from my life was some kind of motif for—what?—my mom leaving?"

She watched me, silent, still.

"Or maybe you think that the three friends from the subway are my family? That each symbolizes someone?"

"Does it?"

I shook my head. I didn't think that. Did I? Hell, you could make something from nothing if you looked at it hard enough, right? Was killing that Chaser a killing of my former self, or a separation from my childhood? And I'd blamed Dave because I couldn't admit to doing it? And what of Caleb, of not being able to kill him . . .

I stopped thinking, because she had got back to her note-making, creating her own conclusion to my story. It was comforting to listen to the sound of her pen scratching across the pages in the folder on her lap. She looked up at me, her eyes settling for a moment on my clenched fists.

I said, "I don't know what you want me to say."

"Say what you need to."

I looked around me, not exactly searching the walls for inspiration, but more as a distraction from her demands to drag more stuff from deep inside me—stuff that I'd left behind, or maybe hadn't even begun to think of. On the wall to the right of the curtained windows, I noticed an old print, a poem titled *The Tyger*.

"What does that mean?" I asked her. "Why a 'fearful symmetry'?"

"That?" she looked at it, smiled, looked at me. "What does it mean to you?"

I remembered how I parroted Felicity when I'd first met her, as I looked at this poster: a tiger walking under a tree, the handwritten poem's verses separated by branches.

"Symmetry might have something to do with beginnings and ends, who knows?" I said. "I wonder, why a *tyger*? I mean, the spelling?"

"Maybe it's not about a tiger, or T-Y tyger, at all." She looked at me closely. "Maybe William Blake intended it as a metaphor."

She went to her bookshelf and pulled out an old,

much-read volume. The cover just tattered red cloth, faded. I thought of Caleb, who loved books. What would he make of this one? She flicked through it but she seemed to know what she was looking for. She handed the book to me, opened at the correct page.

The poem was sweet, simple, yet profound in some way.

"Really, a metaphor?"

"Most stories and poems are."

I smiled at her. She was trying to catch me out. I liked it, this. Could stay all day, going round and round. I handed the book back to her.

"Reminds me of a Poe poem," I said, " 'Alone,' I think it's called . . . The line that sticks with me, is *Of a demon in my view.*"

I looked at her. She sat and watched me, pen poised, expressionless.

"You have an idea what that demon might represent, don't you?"

I nodded.

The doc asked, eager now: "What are you thinking about it?"

I closed my eyes.

"What do you get?" she coaxed.

It was a good question. I wanted to answer it privately before sharing it with the shrink. I thought about my friends, as if they were once again lined up in front of me, come to check that I was okay. You get friendships that never end—eternal, infinite, everlasting—whichever way you look at it.

"Sorry?" I said. Now I looked at her.

"What do you get?" she repeated. "From the Blake poem?"

I looked at the tree, its branches holding the weight of words.

"More than anything," I said, "it makes me wonder if I'm the lamb or the tyger . . ."

"Does it matter?" She wrote as she spoke. "Do you need to be one or the other?"

I shook my head. She looked up at me and I waited for her to put the pen down.

"We're all the same," I said. "We're all capable of anything, everything."

She watched me.

I said, "What does it mean to me? It's just art." I tried to shrug it off. She didn't need to know it all, did she?

"Just?"

"It means we're alive. It means someone out there is thinking, creating, putting something down for us to ponder. To create empathy, if just for a moment— isn't that great?"

I laughed, moved in my chair, leaned forward and, elbows resting on my knees, looked at my useless feet.

"What is it?"

"Nothing."

"No, Jesse. Go on. Tell me." She tried another tack. "Okay, why not tell me about the poem that *does* mean something to you." She nodded. " 'Alone.' "

"What do you want to know about it?"

"How about you start by reciting it for me."

Was she serious? I hadn't come here for a poetry recital. But I found the words easily enough, which was a surprise. I wasn't sure how much stuff from my old life would come back to me, or if it would all seem like some kind of weird dream.

"It starts: *From childhood's hour I have not been, As others . . . as others were . . .*"

I stopped. Stared at the floor, searching. Had I forgotten it? What else had I forgotten . . .

"I think I know that poem," she said. "Want me to—"

"No. I remember it now, all of it."

I smiled, lost in a memory.

She asked, "What is it?"

"It's just, I get it now—it makes sense," I said, seeing not the floor beneath me but a collage of memories playing out. Every one of them a keeper. *"And all I loved, I loved alone . . ."*

ACKNOWLEDGMENTS

Thanks to Jo, Mal, Ben, Chris, Jesse, Sam. Thanks to Mark, Lot, Raff, Kerry, Stephen. Thanks Tony and Natalie. Thanks to Em, Matilda, JJ, Andy. Thanks, Robothams. Thanks to all the readers who sent feedback. Thanks, friends, bloggers, fans. Indebted to Pippa, Steph, Josh, Jon, Sam, Karen. Thanks to all publishing, bookseller, and library staff involved.

Love to Nic.

When writing the first novel, Alone: *Chasers,* I wanted to create a story that was entertaining while being something that would stay with readers long after they've put down the book. The ending has proved a great vehicle for that, and for stimulating word of mouth, judging by the feedback I receive through my website. The initial concept was to write something that showed both the good and the bad that can emerge from human nature in the face of catastrophe, and it gives us hope that even in the worst situations, there are those who will remain strong. I like to think that as we finish the book and go back over what has occurred, the reader will be aware that there is always choice and that "survival" is possible.

Prior to writing *Chasers,* I'd just written a dark thriller about the oil-related corruption in Nigeria and extraordinary rendition, and I was about to delve into the sequel that was set against the water crisis in India. I had really enjoyed talking to school groups with my first two Fox novels, and felt that the tone of that series was moving away from those readers. I had some meetings with publishers to discuss some options of writing a series for teens, wrote some samples (of what they wanted, which was boring, stock-standard boy-spy type material, kind of Fox-lite), and then one day, I thought: "what if everything comes tumbling down?" So, I started writing *Chasers* and was swept away with it so much so that sixteen days later I sent the finished manuscript to my agent.

But let's go back a bit. The idea germed when I was in high school, after I'd read *The Diary of a Young Girl* by Anne Frank, a story that has never left me. That book gave me the concept of how a teenager would go in a war zone and explore how a character coped with her alone time—by communicating with imaginary friends.

At the time, I thought about incorporating this kind of concept into my character Lachlan Fox, who suffers from PTSD, as this was the first novel I started when I was fifteen (which eventually became *Fox-Hunt,* the first in a thriller series published in Australia) but I felt it didn't work with the genre. It's been on the back burner ever since, and I finally found a way of writing this literary technique into *Chasers.* While the three friends of Jesse's are not "imaginary" (as is Tyler Durdan in *Fight Club*), nor are they characters from a book (as is Anne Frank's coping device), these friends of his were "alive," once.

So I had that and the idea that the first book should examine the meaning of being truly alone, isolated, and preyed upon. I wanted to write something that shows us we all have the will we need to survive, whatever the personal circumstance we might bring to the reading, so I explored the story of Jesse via empathy through voice, circumstance, choice, and strong imagery (well, that's the intention!).

I'm a total sucker for postapocalyptic stories—I think the situation is fraught with suspense and ripe for characterization and commentary. I wanted a narrative that would make the reader want to jump into the story and shape it themselves—a quick but gripping read, with a building of tension, so along the way the reader can't help but think, "What would I do?"—and by the final chapter their ideas and assumptions are turned on their head as they rethink the story. Overall, I wanted to write a book that said some things about life, and as a piece of literature would be discussed and remembered by its readers. Anyway, the sum of all this is that I've created a novel that's quite difficult to talk and take questions about, in public, inasmuch as tiptoeing about and not to give away the ending!

Writing the first draft was easy, like I said it was sixteen days of feverish work where the story just poured out, but then making sure I made the narrative work given that Jesse is alone from the prologue on. As a literary device I took away the speech marks when he's "talking" with his friends, as those discussions were something of an internal soliloquy. I think I got away with that device by stating that the prologue and the body of the book was separated by a THEN and NOW. Only at one point in the body of the novel does Jesse speak aloud, and that's to the infected boy at the East River. That was a key moment where he realized that these chasers are not all evil, where he develops real empathy with them, and realizes that we are too quick to judge others. Then, it's not until the final line of the novel that Jesse has the courage to admit to himself, out loud, that he is alone. I designed that to symbolize that we know he will be okay, that he used his friends all this time to survive, and now he'll be all right on his own—he let them go, and with that act he set himself free.

As the series progresses, he meets other survivors. Also, the narrative picks up with action and suspense, so that these three books form a macro-story structure of three acts of a larger picture. We also get some scientific explanations, e.g. the chemical agent of the attack gets a logical explanation. As to "who" perpetrated the attacks . . . well, we get plenty of clues, there's speculation, and there's an "official" explanation at the end of *Quarantine*, but ultimately that is something that I want left for the reader to decide. This is very much an allegorical series and I'm not sure if I want to bore anyone with that yet. . . . I'll wait and see how it's received and discussed at first, and I always rather a reader makes of the book what they will rather than me being didactic about meaning.

Anyway! Both excited and terrified, Jesse soon realizes there may be worse things than being alone. He learns fast that you cannot count on everyone to be

there for you all of the time, that you have to be in-
dependent or else you will most likely not survive
if you were to lose everyone. Trust and fear are big
themes within the story. Although we aren't given
details about the attack that has destroyed the city, I
don't think we need to know what caused it. We already know how wars start, and we are shown how it
ends. Fear? Greed? Lack of trust? All that and more
are explored in the relationships of characters throughout the series.

Jesse is a likable narrator, with a natural voice and a
well-developed personality. It's easy to sympathize
with him based on his situation alone, but he is all the
more admirable for refusing to give up even in the
most desperate circumstances. He deals with his problems with intelligence and courage, but still has those
moments of carelessness and fear that make him human. Readers will be on his side from the beginning,
even as they struggle to imagine how they would feel
in his place. Though his final triumph involves some
loss, it's clear he will persevere and find a way to survive on his own, which makes the ending satisfying.

The only research I did was in relation to Jesse's
psychological condition, and that involved reading
books and articles and talking to my psychiatrist. The
book has many elements from my own life, and I've
been to the places that Jesse goes to and sees, albeit
the Manhattan I know is still (mostly) standing. I see
this as a YA crossover and not gender specific, although I was conscious of writing a story that young

male readers would enjoy reading. I'm sure there are some good books being published out there with similar appeal, but to me there seemed to be heaps of straight-up action/adventure books for boys and not much else. Alone was my answer to that.